The Flight To

Jules Gabriel Verne

Volume 31 of 54 in the

"Voyages Extraordinaires"

First published in 1887.

2012 Reprint by Kassock Bros. Publishing Co.

Printed in the United States Of America

Cover Illustration By Isaac M. Kassock

ISBN: 1483999777
ISBN-13: 978-1483999777

Jules Gabriel Verne (1828-1905)

The Extraordinary Voyages
of
Jules Verne
~

Table of Contents

THE FLIGHT TO FRANCE

CHAPTER I

My name is Natalis Delpierre. I was born in 1761, at Grattepanche, a village in Picardy. My father was a farm laborer. He worked on the estate of the Marquis d'Estrelle. My mother did her best to help him. My sisters and I followed our mother's example.

My father never possessed any property. He was precentor at the church, and had a powerful voice that could be heard even in the grave-yard. The voice was almost all I inherited from him.

My father and mother worked hard. They both died the same year, 1779. God has their souls in His keeping!

Of my two sisters, Firminie, the eldest, at this time was forty-five; the younger, Irma, was forty, and I was thirty- one. When our parents died, Firminie married a man at Escarbotin, Benoin Fanthomme, a working blacksmith, who, however clever he might be, was never able to start in business on his own account. In 1781 they had had three children, and a fourth came a few years later. My sister Irma remained unmarried. Neither on her nor on the Fanthommes could I depend for my living. I had to make my own way in the world. In my old days I could then come back to help them.

My father died first; my mother six months afterward. It was a great blow to me. But such is destiny! We must lose those we love as well as those we do not love. Let us, however, strive to be among those that are loved when our turn comes to depart.

The paternal inheritance amounted, when all was paid, to one hundred and fifty livres — the savings of sixty years of work. This was divided between my sisters and me.

At eighteen I thus found myself with practically nothing. But I was healthy, strongly built, accustomed to hard work, and I had a splendid voice. But I did not know how to read or write. I did not learn to do so till later, as you will see. And when one does not begin early at those things, the task is a hard one. I have always felt the effects of this in trying to express my ideas — as will appear clearly enough in what follows.

What was to become of me? Was I to continue in my father's trade? A hopeless lookout, indeed! And one I did not care to try. Something happened which decided my fate.

A cousin of the Marquis d'Estrelle, the Comte de Linois, arrived one day at Grattepanche. He was an officer, a captain in the Regiment de la Fere. He had two months' leave, and had come to pass them with his relative. There were great huntings of the boar and the fox, with the hounds and without; there were parties to which the great world were invited, and many fine folks, to say nothing of the wife of the marquis, who was as beautiful as any of them.

Among them all I only had eyes for Captain de Linois — an officer very free in his manners, who would speak with anybody. The idea came to me to be a soldier. Is it not best when you have to live by your arms, that your arms should be fixed to a solid body? Besides, with good conduct, courage, and a little by luck, there is no reason to stop on the road, particularly if you start with the left foot and march at a good pace.

There are many people who imagine that before 1789, a private soldier, the son of a tradesman or peasant, could not become an officer. It is an error. With perseverance and good conduct he could without very much trouble become a sub-officer. That was the first step. Then, after he had acted as such for ten years in time of peace or five years in time of war, he was in a position to obtain his epaulet. From sergeant he became lieutenant, from lieutenant, captain. Then — but halt! we must not go further than that. The outlook is promising enough!

The Comte de Linois, during the shooting-parties, had often noticed my strength and activity. Likely enough I was not so good as a dog for scent or intelligence, but on grand days there were none of the beaters who could teach me anything, and I scampered about as if my breeches were on fire.

3

"You look like a stout-spirited fellow," said the Comte de Linois to me one day.

"Yes, sir."

"And strong in the arms?"

"I can lift three hundred and twenty."

"I congratulate you."

And that was all. But it did not rest there, as you will see.

At that time there was a curious custom in the army. The way in which soldiers were enlisted was this: Every year recruiters were sent out into the country places. They made men drink more than was good for them; and got them to sign a paper if they knew how to write, or to mark it with a cross if they did not. The cross was as good as a signature. Then they were given a couple of hundred livres, which were drunk almost as soon as they were pocketed, and then they were off to have their heads broken for the good of their country.

That style of proceeding did not suit me. If I wished to serve my country I did not wish to sell myself to it; and I fancy that all who have any dignity or respect for themselves will be of the same opinion.

Well, in those days, when an officer went away on leave, it was his duty to bring back with him on his return one or two recruits. And the sub-officers were under the same obligation. The bounty then varied from twenty to twenty-five livres.

I was not ignorant of all this, and I had my plan. When the leave of the Comte de Linois had nearly expired, I went boldly to him and asked him to take me as a recruit.

"You?" said he.

"Me, sir."

"How old are you?"

"Eighteen."

4

"And you would be a soldier?"

"If it pleases you."

"It is not if it pleases me, but if it pleases you."

"It pleases me."

"Ah! the charms of the twenty livres?"

"No, the wish to serve my country. And as I should be ashamed to sell myself, I shall not take your twenty livres."

"What is your name?"

"Natalis Delpierre."

"Well, Natalis, you shall come with me."

"I am delighted to go with you, captain."

"And if you choose to follow me you will go far."

"I will follow you wherever the drum beats."

"I tell you beforehand that I am going to leave La Fere, to go aboard ship. You do not dislike the sea?"

"Not at all."

"Good! you will cross it. Do you know that a war is on to drive the English out of America?", "What is America?"

And in truth I had never heard tell of America!

"A deuce of a country," said Captain de Linois, "which is fighting for its independence. For the last two years the Marquis de Lafayette has been making himself talked about over there. Last year King Louis XVI. promised to send soldiers to help the Americans. The Comte de Rochambeau is going with Admiral de Grasse and six thousand men. I am going with him to the New World, and if you will come with me we shall go and deliver America."

"Go and deliver America!"

And that, not to be long over it, is how I came to be engaged in the expeditionary force of Comte de Rochambeau, and landed at Newport in 1780.

There for three years I remained far away from France.

I saw General Washington — a giant of five feet eleven, with large feet, large hands, a blue coat turned up with wash-leather, and a black cockade. I saw the sailor Paul Jones on board his ship the "Bonhomme Richard." I saw General Anthony Wayne, who was known as the Madman. I fought in several encounters, not without making the sign of the cross with my first cartridge. I took part in the siege of Yorktown, in Virginia, where, after a memorable defense, Lord Cornwallis surrendered to Washington. I returned to France in 1783. I had escaped without a scratch; and I was a private soldier as before. What would you have? I did not know how to read!

The Comte de Linois came back with us. He wished me to enter the Regiment de la Fere, in which he was to resume his rank. But I had an idea of serving in the cavalry. I had an instinctive love of horses, and for me to become a mounted officer of infantry I should have to pass through many steps, very many steps!

I knew that the uniform of the foot-soldier was a tempting one, and very becoming, with the queue, the powder, the side curls, and the white cross-belts. But what would you have? The horse, the horse for me; and after much thinking I found my trade as a horseman. And I thanked the Comte de Linois, who had recommended me to his friend Colonel Lostanges, and I joined the Eoyal Picardy Regiment.

I loved it, this splendid regiment, and you will pardon me if I speak of it with a tenderness that is ridiculous perhaps. In it I served nearly all my time, thought much of my superiors, whose protection was never denied me, and who, as they say in our village, put their shoulders to the wheel for me.

And besides, a few years later, in 1792, the Regiment de la Ffire behaved so strangely in its dealings with the Austrian general,

Beaulieu, that I am not sorry I left it. I will say no more about it, but return to the Royal Picardy. No finer regiment could be seen. It became as it were a family to me. I remained faithful to it until it was disbanded. I was happy in it. I whistled all its fanfares and drum-calls, for I always had the bad habit of whistling through my teeth.

For eight years I did nothing but go from garrison to garrison. Not an occasion offered itself for a shot at an enemy. Bah! Such a life is not without its charms for those who know how to make the best of it. And besides, to see the country was something for a Picard picardizing as I was. After America, a little of France, while we were waiting to cover step on the main roads across Europe. We were at Sarrelouis in '85; at Angers in '88; in '91 in Brittany, at Josselin, at Pontivy, at Ploermel, at Nantes, with Colonel Serre de Gras; in '92 at Charleville, with Colonel de Wardner, Colonel de Lostende, Colonel la Roque; and in '93 with Colonel le Comte.

But I forgot to say that on the 1st of January, 1791, there came into force a law which changed the composition of the army. The Royal Picardy became the 20th Regiment of the cavalry of the line. This organization lasted till 1803. But the regiment did not lose its old title. It remained the Royal Picardy, although for some years there had been no king in France.

It was under Colonel Serre de Gras that I was made a corporal, to my great satisfaction. Under Colonel de Wardner I was made quartermaster, and that pleased me more. I had had thirteen years' service, been through a campaign, and received no wound. That was a great advantage, as you may suppose. I could not rise higher, for, I repeat it, I could not read or write. And I was always whistling; and it is not quite the thing for a sub-officer to go about like a blackbird.

Quartermaster Natalis Delpierre! That was something to be proud of; something impressive! And deep was my gratitude to Colonel de Wardner, although he was as rough as barley-bread, and it was "attend to the word of command "with him.

That day the men of my company fusilladed my knapsack, and I put on my sleeves the lace which could never rise to my elbow.

We were in garrison at Charleville when I asked for two months' leave, which was granted to me. It is the history of this leave that I am going to relate faithfully. These are my reasons for doing so.

Since I have retired from soldiering I have often had to tell the story of my campaigns during our evening meetings at the village of Grattepanche.

Friends have misunderstood me, or not understood me at all. Some have thought I was on the right when I was on the left, some that I was on the left when I was on the right. And thence have come disputes which have not ended over two glasses of cider or two coifees — two small pots. Above all, what happened to me during my leave in Germany they seem never to understand. And, as I have learned to write, I think it best to take up my pen and tell the story of my leave. I have thus set to work, although I am seventy years old this very day. But my memory is good, and when I look back I can see clearly enough. This recital is thus dedicated to my friends at Gratte-

panche, to the Ternisiens, Bettemboses, Irondarts, Pointe- fers, Quennehens, and others, who will, I hope, leaVe off disputing on the subject.

It was on the 7th of June, 1792, then, that I obtained my leave. There were then certain rumors of war with Germany, but they were still very vague. It was said that Europe looked with an evil eye on what was passing in France. The king was at the Tuileries, it is true. But the 10th of August was being scented from afar, and a breeze of republicanism was sweeping over the country.

Had I been prudent I should not have asked for leave. But I had business in Germany, in Prussia even. In case of war I should find it difficult to get back to my post. But what would you have? You can not ring the church bell and walk in the procession at the same time. And, although my leave was for two months, I had decided to cut it short if necessary. All the same I hoped the worst would not happen.

Now, to finish with what concerns me, and what concerns my gallant regiment, this is what in a few words I have to say.

First you will see how it was I began to learn to read, and then to write; and thus gained a chance of becoming officer, general, marshal of France, count, duke, prince, like Ney, Davout, or Murat, during the wars of the Empire. In reality I did not get beyond the rank of captain; but that is not so bad for the son of a peasant, a peasant himself.

As for the Royal Picardy, a very few lines will suffice to finish its story.

It had in 1793, as I have said, M. le Comte for its colonel; and it was in this year, owing to the decree of the 21st of February, that the regiment became a demi- brigade. It then went through the campaigns with the army of the North, and the army of the Sambre and Meuse, until 1797. It distinguished itself at the battles of Lincelles and Courtray, where I was a lieutenant. Then, after staying in Paris from 1797 till 1800, it joined the army of Italy, and distinguished itself at Marengo in surrounding six battalions of Austrian grenadiers, who laid down their arms after the rout of a Hungarian regiment. In this affair I was wounded by a ball in the hip, which did not trouble me much, for it caused me to get my captaincy.

The Royal Picardy being disbanded in 1803, I entered the dragoons, and served in all the wars of the Empire until I retired in 1815.

Now, when I speak of myself, it is only to relate what happened during my leave in Germany. But do not forget that I am not a well-educated man. I hardly know how to tell these things. And if there escape me a few expressions or turns of phrase that betray the Picard, you must excuse them. I can not speak in another way. I will get along as fast as I can, and never stand with two feet in a shoe. I will tell you all, and if I ask you to allow me to express myself without reserve, I hope you will reply, "You are quite at liberty to do so, sir!"

CHAPTER II

At the time I speak of, as I have read in history-books, Germany was divided into ten circles. Later on new arrangements were made which established the Confederation of the Rhine in 1806 under the protectorate of Napoleon; and then came the Germanic Confederation of 1815. One of these circles, comprising the electorates of Saxony aud Brandenburg, then bore the name of Upper Saxony.

This electorate of Brandenburg became later on one of the provinces of Prussia, and was divided into two districts, the district of Brandenburg and the district of Potsdam. I say this so that you will know where to find the little town of Belzingen, which is in the district of Potsdam — in the north-western part — a few leagues from the frontier.

It was on this frontier that I arrived on the 16th of June, after traversing the one hundred and fifty leagues that separated it from France. I had taken nine days on the journey, and that will show you that the communications were not easy. I had worn out more nails in my boots than in horse's shoes or wheels of carriages — or rather carts, to be more correct. I was not quite reduced to my eggs, as they say in Picardy, but I had not saved much from my pay, and wished to be as economical as possible. Fortunately, during my stay in garrison on the frontier I had picked up a few words of German, which came in useful in getting me out of difficulties. It was, however, difficult to hide that I was a Frenchman; and consequently more than a passing look was given to me as I went by. I took care not to say that I was Quartermaster Natal is Del- pierre. You will think me wise under the circumstances, when a war was threatened between us and Prussia and Austria, the whole of Germany in fact.

At the frontier of the district I had a pleasant surprise. I was on foot. I was walking toward an inn to get my breakfast, the inn of Ecktvende — in French the Tourne Coin. After a coldish night a beautiful morning. The seven-o'clock sun was drinking the dew of the meadows. There was quite a swarm of birds on the beeches, oaks, elms, and birches. The country was but little cultivated. Many of the fields lay fallow. The climate is a severe one in these parts.

At the door of the Ecktvende a small cariole was waiting, drawn by a wiry-looking nag, able perhaps to do a couple of leagues an hour if there were not too many hills.

With it was a woman, a tall, strong, well-built woman, with a corsage with laced straps, straw hat with yellow ribbons, and red and violet banded skirt, all well fitting and very clean, as if it was a Sunday or holiday costume.

And it was a holiday for the woman, although it was not Sunday.

She looked at me, and I looked at her looking at me.

Suddenly she opened her arms, and ran toward me, exclaiming: "Natalis!"

"Irma!"

It was my sister. She had recognized me. Truly women have better eyes for remembrances that come from the heart — or rather quicker eyes. It was thirteen years since we had seen each other. How well she had kept herself! She reminded me of our mother, with her large, quick eyes, and her black hair just beginning to turn gray on the temples. I kissed her on her two plump cheeks, reddened by the morning breeze, and I leave you to imagine what smacks she gave mine!

It was for her, to see her, that I had obtained my leave. I was uneasy at her being out of France now the clouds had begun to gather. A French woman among the Germans would be in an awkward position should war be declared. It would be better for her to be in her own country; and, if my sister chose, I intended to take her back with me. To do that she would have to leave her mistress, Mme. Keller, and I doubted if she would consent. That was to be inquired into.

"How glad I am to see you, Natalis," she said; "to find ourselves together again so far from Picardy! It feels as though you had brought some of our native air with you! It is time enough since we saw each other!"

"Thirteen years, Irma!"

"Yes, thirteen years! Thirteen years of separation! That is a long time, Natalis!"

"Dear Irma!" I replied.

And there we were, my sister and I, with arms linked together walking up and down the road.

"And how are you?" asked I.

"Always pretty well, Natalis. And you?"

"The same!"

"And you are a quartermaster! There is an honor for the family!"

"Yes, Irma, and a great honor! Who would have thought that the little goose-minder of Grattepanche would become a quartermaster! But we must not talk about it too much."

"Why not?"

"Because to tell everybody I am a soldier would not be without its inconveniences in this country When rumors of war are flying about, it is a serious matter for a Frenchman to find himself in Germany. No! I am your brother, Monsieur Nothing-at-all, who has come to see his sister."

"Good, Natalis; we shall be silent about it, I promise you."

"That will be best, for German spies have good ears."

"Do not be uneasy."

"And if you will take my advice, Irma, I will take you back with me to France."

A look of sorrow came into my sister's eyes, as she gave me the answer I expected: "Go away from Madame Keller, Natalis! when you will see and understand that I can not leave her alone."

I understood this as it was, and I thought it best to postpone what I had to say.

And then Irma resumed her bright eyes and sweet voice, asking me for the news of the country and our people.

"And our sister Firminie?"

"She is well. I have had news of her from our neighbor Letocard, who came to Charleville two months ago. You remember Letocard?"

"The wheelwright's son?"

"Yes! You know, or you do not know, that he is married to a Matifas!"

"The daughter of the old woman at Fouencamps?"

"Herself. He told me that our sister does not complain of her health. Ah! they have to work, and work hard, at Escarbotin! They have four children now, and the last one — a troublesome boy! Luckily, she has an honest husband, a good workman, and not much of a drunkard, except on Mondays. But she has had much trouble in her time."

"She is getting old."

"She is five years older than you, Irma, and fourteen older than I am! That is something! But what would you have? She is a brave woman, and so are you."

"Oh! Natalis! If I have known sorrow, it has only been the sorrow of others. Since I left Grattepanche I have had no trouble of my own. But to see people suffer near you when you can do nothing — "

My sister's face clouded again. She turned the conversation.

"And your journey?" she asked.

"All right! The weather has been good enough, for the season. And, as you see, my legs are pretty strong. Besides, who cares for fatigue, when he is sure of a welcome when he arrives?"

"As you are, Natalis, and they will give you a good welcome, and they will love you in the family as they love me."

"Excellent Madame Keller! Do you know, sister, I shall not recognize her. For me she is still the daughter of Monsieur and Madame Acloque, the good people of Saint Sauflieu. When she was married, twenty-five years ago, I was only a boy. But father and mother used to tell us about her."

"Poor woman," said Irma, "she is much changed. What a wife she has been, Natalis; and what a mother she is still!"

. "And her son?"

"The best of sons, who has bravely set to work to take the place of his father, who died fifteen months ago."

"Brave Monsieur Jean!"

"He adores his mother; he lives only for her, as she lives only for him."

"I have never seen him, Irma, and I am impatient to know him. It seems that I love the young man already."

"There is nothing astonishing in that, Natalis."

"Then let us be off."

"Come along, then."

"In a minute! How far are we from Belzingen?"

"Five long leagues."

"Bah!" was my answer. "If I was alone I would do that in three hours. But we must — "

"I will do it quicker than you, Natalis."

14

"On your legs?"

"No, on my horse's legs."

And Irma pointed to the cariole at the inn door.

"Did you come to look for me in that cariole?"

"Yes, Natalis; to bring you to Belzingen. I started early this morning, and I was here at seven o'clock to the minute. And if the letter you sent had come sooner, I should have gone further to meet you."

"Oh! there would have been no good in that. Come, let us get off. You have nothing to pay at the inn? I have a few kreutzers — "

"Thanks, Natalis, it is done, and all we have to do is to start."

"While we were talking, the innkeeper of the Ecktvende, leaning against the door, seemed to be listening, without taking much notice of us.

I thought this unsatisfactory. Perhaps it would have been better for us to have spoken to each other further off. He was a fat man, quite a mountain, with a disagreeable face, eyes deeply set, folded eyelids, small nose, and a large mouth, as if he had eaten his soup with a sword when he was young.

After all, we had not said anything that could damage us. Perhaps he had not heard all that passed. If he did not know French he would not know that I came from France.

We got into the cariole. The innkeeper saw us leave without making the slightest move.

I took the reins. I started the nag briskly; we spun along like the wind in January. That did not keep us from talking, and Irma told me how matters stood. And from what I knew already, and what she told me, I will now say something about the Keller family.

CHAPTER III

Mme. Keller was born in 1747, and was then forty-five years old. A native of Saint Sauflieu, as I have said, she belonged to a family of small proprietors. M. and Mme. Acloque, her father and mother, had a very modest competence, but saw it grow less year by year. They died, one shortly after the other, in 1765. Their daughter remained in the care of an old aunt, whose death would soon have left her alone in the world.

It was under these circumstances that she was found by M. Keller, who had come to Picardy on business. He established himself for eighteen months at Amiens, where he was engaged as a forwarding agent for goods and merchandise. He was a man of serious mind, good bearing, intelligent and active. At that time we had not that repulsion toward the German race, which grew later out of national hatred fostered by thirty years of war. M. Keller possessed a certain amount of fortune, which could not but be increased by his zeal and business capacity. He asked Mlle. Acloque to become his wife.

Mlle. Acloque hesitated, because she would have to leave Saint Sauflieu and the Picardy she loved. And would she not by this marriage cease to be a French woman? But then all she possessed was a small house which she would have to 'sell. What would become of her after this last sacrifice? And Mme. Dufrenay, the old aunt, feeling that death was approaching, and alarmed at the position in which her niece would find herself, pressed her to consent.

Mlle. Acloque consented. The marriage took place at Saint Sauflieu. Mme. Keller left Picardy a few months later and followed her husband beyond the frontier. She never repented the choice she had made. Her husband was good to her and she was good to him. Always attentive to her, he so won her love that she seldom thought of having lost her nationality. The marriage was one of reason and expediency, and yet it turned out happy, which such marriages rarely did then or do in our time.

A year afterward, at Belzingen, Mme. Keller had a son. She resolved to devote herself entirely to the education of this child, who will fill a prominent part in our story.

It was some time after the birth of this son, about 1771, that my sister Irma, then nineteen, went into service at the Kellers. Mme. Keller had known her as a child. Our father had been occasionally employed by M. Acloque, whose wife and daughter took an interest in us. From Orattepanche to Saint Sauflieu is not very far. Mlle. Acloque often met my sister, kissed her, made her presents, and admitted her to a friendship which the truest devotion was one day to repay.

When she heard of the death of our father and mother, which left us almost without means, Mme. Keller thought of taking Irma into her service. Irma was then in the service of a family at Saint Sauflieu, but she gladly accepted the offer — and she never had cause to repent doing so.

M. Keller was of French descent. About a century before, the Kellers lived in French Lorraine. They were well-to-do commercial people of marked ability. And they were prospering, when there occurred that grave incident which changed the future of thousands of the most industrious families of France.

The Kellers were Protestants, much attached to their religion, whom no question of self-interest could induce to be renegades. This was clearly shown when the Edict of Nantes was revoked in 1685. Like many others, they had the choice of quitting their country or changing their faith. Like many others they preferred exile.

Manufacturers, artisans, workmen of all sorts, agriculturists, departed from France to enrich England, the Low Countries, Switzerland, Germany, and particularly Brandenburg. There they received a hearty welcome from the Elector of Prussia and Potsdam, to Berlin, Magdeburg, Stettin, and Frankfort-on-the-Oder. Twenty-five thousand natives of Metz, I am told, went to found the flourishing colonies of Stettin and Potsdam.

The Kellers then abandoned Lorraine, not without hope of return. Meanwhile they took up their abode with the stranger. New relations grew up, new interests arose. Years rolled by and still they remained.

At this time Prussia, the foundation of which as a kingdom dates only from 1701, possessed on the Rhine only the duchy of Cleves, the county of La Marck, and a part of Gueldres. It was in this last province that the Kellers sought refuge. There they founded factories, and got back the trade interrupted by the iniquitous and deplorable revocation of the Edict of Henry IV. Generation followed generation, and alliances were formed with the new countrymen, and gradually the French refugees became German subjects.

About 1760 one of the Kellers left Gueldres to establish himself in the little town of Belzingen, in the center of the circle of Upper Saxony which comprised a part of Prussia. He succeeded in his enterprise, and was thus enabled to offer Mlle. Acloque the comfortable home she could not find at Saint Sauflieu. It was at Belzingen that her son had come into the world, a Prussian on his father's side, although through his mother French blood flowed in his veins.

And, I say it with emotion that still makes my heart leap, he was French to the soul, this brave young man in whom his mother's spirit lived again. She had fed him on her milk. In his first childish words he had lisped in French. It was not "mamma" he said, but "maman!" Although Mme. Keller and my sister Irma soon learned to speak German, French was the language usually heard in the house at Belzingen, and French was the first language he heard.

The boy was rocked to sleep with the songs of our country. His father never thought of objecting. On the contrary, was not the language of his ancestors that Lorraine tongue which is so French, and the purity of which the neighborhood of the German frontier has not been able to alter?

And it was not only with her milk, but with her own ideas that Mme. Keller had nourished the child. She was deeply attached to her native country. She had never given up the hope of one day returning to it. She never concealed the fact that her joy would be great when she could again look over the old lands of Picardy. M. Keller in no way objected to this. When his fortune was made he would willingly leave Germany and settle in France, but he must work a few more years yet to make sure of a proper position for his wife and child. Unfortunately, death had surprised him about fifteen months before I met my sister.

Such were the things she told me as we rolled along in the cariole to Belzingen. This unexpected death had delayed the return of the family to France — and what misfortunes followed! When M. Keller died he was engaged in a lawsuit against the Prussian Government. For two or three years, as contractor of stores for the government, he had embarked not only his own capital, but certain funds that had been intrusted to him. From his first receipts he had been able to pay back his partners, but the bulk of the amount, equal to almost his entire fortune, remained owing to him and there were no hopes of a speedy settlement. The officials disputed with M. Keller, and raised difficulties of all kinds, and he had at last to appeal to the judges at Berlin. The lawsuit dragged on.

It is not a wise thing to go to law with a government in any country. The Prussian judges showed unmistakable ill-will toward him, although M. Keller had faithfully fulfilled his engagements, for he was an honest man. A sum of twenty thousand florins was in question — a fortune in those days — and the loss of the lawsuit would be his ruin. Had it not been for the delay in this matter, the position of affairs at Belzingen would have been settled for the best, and Mme. Keller's wish to return to France after her husband's death would have been accomplished.

This is what my sister told me. Her own place in the family can be imagined. She had brought up the child almost from his birth, and loved him with truly maternal affection. She was not looked upon as a servant in the house, but as a companion, an humble and modest friend. She was one of the family, treated as they were, and devoted to them. If the Kellers left Germany, it was with great joy she would go with them. If they remained at Belzingen she would remain with them.

"Separate me from Madame Keller! It would be like death to me!" said Irma.

I saw that nothing would persuade my sister to return with me, so long as her mistress was forced to remain at Belzingen. But to see her in the midst of a country ready to rise against ours gave me great uneasiness, and pardonably so, for if a war began it would not be a short one.

When Irma had given me all the news about the Kellers, she asked: "You are going to stay with us during the whole of your leave?"

"Yes, all my leave, if I can."

"Well, Natalis, it is riot unlikely that you will be asked to a wedding."

"Whose? Monsieur Jean's?"

"Yes."

"And who is he to marry? A German?"

"No, Natalis, and that is why we are pleased. If his mother married a German, he is going to marry a French woman."

"A good-looking one?"

"Beautiful as an angel."

"I am glad of that, Irma."

"And so are we. But are you never going to get married, Natalis?"

"I!"

"Are you married?"

"Yes, Irma."

"And to whom?"

"To my country, sister! And what else can a soldier want?"

CHAPTER IV

Belzingen is a little town not quite twenty leagues from Berlin, and near the village of Hagelberg, where in 1813 the French fought the Prussian Landwehr. It is picturesquely situated at the foot of Flameng, and is commanded by its ridge. Its trade is in horses, cattle, flax, clover, and cereals.

My sister and I arrived there about ten o'clock in the morning. In a few minutes the cariole had stopped before a house that was very clean and attractive, though unpretending It was Mme. Keller's.

In those parts you would think you were in Holland. The country people have long bluish coats, scarlet waistcoats, with a tall thick collar that would protect them splendidly from a saber-cut; the women have double and triple petticoats. Their caps, with white wings, would make them look like Sisters of Charity, were it not for the bright-colored dresses that fit tight to the figure, and the corsage of black velvet, which has nothing about it of the nun. At least that is what I saw as I went along.

The welcome I received may be imagined. Was I not Irma's own brother? I saw at once that her position in this family was not inferior to what she had told me. Mme. Keller honored me with an affectionate smile, and M. Jean with a hearty shake of the hand. My being a Frenchman stood me in good part.

"Monsieur Delpierre," he said to me, "my mother and I expect you to pass all your leave among us. A few weeks is not much to give to the sister whom you have not seen for thirteen years."

"To give to my sister, to your mother, and to yourself!" said I. "I have not forgotten how good your family has been to mine, and it was a great pleasure to us for Irma to have been taken into your service."

I confess that I had prepared this little compliment, so as not to appear quite a stupid at my introduction. But it was not wanted. With such people you could say what your heart told you.

Looking at Mme. Keller, I recognized the features which were graven on my memory. Her beauty as a girl did not seem to have changed with her years. In her youth the seriousness of her look was already striking, and it was the same now. If her dark hair had grown white in places, her eyes had not lost their former vivacity. Fire still burned in them, in spite of the tears which had bathed them since the death of her husband. She bore herself calmly. She knew how to listen. She was not one of those women who chatter like a one-eyed magpie, or buzz like a bee. And frankly I do not like such folks. You felt that Mme. Keller was a person of sense, knowing how to think before she spoke or acted, and understanding how to deal with business matters.

And, as I soon found, she rarely left the domestic hearth. She did not go visiting. She avoided acquaintances. She stayed much at home. That is what I like in a woman. I do not think much of those who, like fiddlers, are always best outside the house.

One thing gave me great pleasure. This was that, without despising German customs, Mme. Keller had retained some of our customs in Picardy. The arrangement of the house reminded you of the house at Saint Sauflieu. In the way the furniture was arranged, and the meals prepared, you would have thought you were in Picardy. I made a note of this in my memory.

M. Jean was then twenty-four years old. He was above the middle height, with brown hair and mustaches, and eyes so dark that they seemed to be black. If he was a German, he had nothing of the Teutonic stiffness. His disposition was frank, open, sympathetic, attractive. He was much like his mother. Naturally serious as she was, he was obliging, and always ready to be of service. I quite took to him as soon as I set eyes on him. If he wanted a devoted friend he would find one in Natalis Delpierre.

I may add that he knew our language as well as if he had been brought up in our country. Did he know German? Yes, evidently, and knew it well. But you had to ask for it, as you had to ask I know not what Queen of Prussia who habitually spoke French. And, besides, he was above all things interested in French affairs. He liked our countrymen, he sought them out, and assisted them. The news from France was his favorite subject of conversation.

He belonged to the class of manufacturers and merchants, and as such suffered a good deal from the arrogance of functionaries and military people, as do all young men of business who are not in the government service.

It was a pity that Jean Keller was only half a Frenchman! I say what I think and what I feel. If I was not enraptured with the Germans it was because I had seen them at close quarters when in garrison on the frontier. In the upper classes, even when they are polite, as all ought to be, their natural haughtiness is always noticeable. I do not deny their good qualities, but the French have others as good. And my journey into Germany gave me no reason for changing my opinion.

At his father's death M. Jean, then studying at the University of Gottingen, had had to take over the business. Mme. Keller had found in him an active, intelligent, hardworking assistant. But that was not the limit of his powers. Outside his business he was a well-informed man — at least my sister said so, for I am no judge myself. He was fond of books; he was fond of music. He had a splendid voice, not so strong as mine, but more agreeable. Each to his trade. When I shouted to my men, "Forward! Quick-march! Halt!" — particularly "Halt!" — they had no trouble in hearing me. But let us get back to M. Jean. If I had to listen to myself I should never end with his praises. You will judge for yourselves; but what you should remember now is, that after his father's death, the whole burden of the business fell on him, and that he had to work hard, for matters were very complicated. He never deviated from his object to clear up the difficulties and retire from the business. Unfortunately this lawsuit against the government seemed to have no end. It had to be pursued assiduously, and in order that nothing might be neglected, he had to go often to Berlin. On it the future of the Keller family depended. After all, the justice of their claim was so undeniable that they could not fail, no matter how great might be the ill-will of the judges.

At noon that day we dined at the same table. We were a family party. That is the way they treated me. I sat next to Mme. Keller. My sister Irma occupied her usual place near M. Jean, who sat opposite to me.

We talked of my journey, of the difficulties I had met with on the way, of the state of the country. I guessed the anxiety of Mme. Keller and her son with regard to what was coming with this march of troops toward the frontier of France — Austrian troops, as well as Prussian troops. Their interests would be endangered for a long time if war broke out.

But it was best not to speak of such sad things at our first dinner. And M. Jean changed the conversation, and I was shut up.

"And how about your wars, Natalis?" he asked. " You have been under fire in America. You met there the Marquis de Lafayette, the heroic Frenchman who devoted his life and fortune to the cause cf independence!"

"Yes, Monsieur Jean."

"And did you see Washington?"

"As close as I see you; a splendid man, with large feet, and large hands — a giant!"

Evidently that is what struck me most about the American general.

Then I had to tell them what I knew about Yorktown, and how Comte de Rochambeau had properly beaten Lord Cornwallis.

"And since you came back to France," asked M. Jean, "you have not been to war?"

"Not once," answered I. "The Royal Picardy has only gone from garrison to garrison. We have been very busy — "

"I believe it, Natalis, and so busy that you have never had time to send us any news, or to write a word to your sister!"

I turned very red at that. Irma looked rather annoyed too. But I made up my mind. There was nothing to be ashamed of, after all.

"Monsieur Jean," said I, "if I have not written to my sister it is because that when I had time to write I was crippled in both arms!"

"Do you not know how to write, then?" said M. Jean.

"No, I am sorry to say."

"Nor read?"

"No! When I was a child, even if my father and mother had had a few sous to pay for me to be taught, we had no school-master at Grattepanche or in the neighborhood. Since then I have always lived knapsack on back, musket on shoulder, and there has not been much time to study between the halting-places. That is why a quartermaster thirty-one years old does not yet know how to read and write!"

"We — we will teach you, Natalis," said Mme. Keller.

"You, madame?"

"Yes," said M. Jean. "My mother and I. We will both see about it. You have two months' leave?"

"Two months."

"And you intend to spend them here?"

"If I am not in the way."

"You in the way?" said Mme. Keller. "You, Irma's brother!"

"Dear mistress," said my sister, "when Natalis knows you better he will not have such ideas as that."

"You are to live here as if you were at home," said M. Jean.

"At home!... Wait, Monsieur Keller!... I have never had a home..."

"Well, at your sister's home, if you like that better. I say again, stay here as long as you like. And in your two months' leave I will undertake to teach you to read. Writing comes afterward."

I did not know how to thank him enough.

"But, Monsieur Jean," said I, "is not all your time occupied?"

"Two hours in the morning, two hours in the evening, that will be enough. I will set you your lessons, and you must do them."

"I will help you, Natalis," said Irma, " for I know how to read and write a little."

"So I should think," added M. Jean. "She was my mother's best pupil."

What was I to reply to a proposition made in such a way?

"I am willing, Monsieur Jean; I am willing, Madame Keller; and if I do not do my lessons properly you must punish me."

M. Jean answered: "You see, my dear Natalis, it is necessary that a man should know how to read and write. Think of what the poor people who have never learned can not know! What darkness there must be in their brains! What a void there must be in their intelligence! It is as bad as being without a limb! And you can not rise in rank. You are a quartermaster, that is well enough, but how are you to go higher? How are you to become lieutenant, captain, colonel? You will remain where you are, and it ought not to be that ignorance should stop you on your road."

"It will not be ignorance that will stop me, Monsieur Jean," said I, "but the regulation. To us of the people there is no going above the rank of captain."

"At present, Natalis, that is possible. But the revolution of 1789 proclaimed equality in France, and the old prejudices will disappear. Among you, now, all men are equal. Be then the equal of those who are

27

educated, to rise where education will lead you. Equality! It is a word that Germany does not yet know! Is it not so?"

"It is so, Monsieur Jean."

"Well, we will begin this very day; and in a week you will be at the last letter of your ABO. We have finished dinner. Come and have a walk. When we come back we will set to work."

And. that is how I began to learn to read at Mme. Keller's. Could there be better people than these?

CHAPTER V

We had a good walk along the road rising toward Hagelberg on the Brandenburg side. We paid more attention to our talk than to looking about us. In fact there is nothing much to see.

But I noticed all the time that people eyed me curiously. But what of that? A new face in a small town is an event. I also noticed that M. Keller seemed to be held in general esteem. Among those we met or passed there were few who did not know him. And there was much lifting of the hat which I thought best to acknowledge politely, although it was not personally addressed to me. It would not do to fail in old French politeness.

What did M. Jean talk about during our walk? Ah! Of that which troubled his people more than anything — of this lawsuit which never finished.

He told me the whole affair. The goods contracted for had been delivered at the dates agreed upon. M. Keller, being a Prussian, had fulfilled all the required conditions, and the payment legitimately and honestly earned ought to have been made to him without protest. If ever a lawsuit ought to have been won it was this. Under the circumstances the agents of the government had acted like scoundrels.

"But wait," said I; "these agents are not your judges. They will do you justice, and it is impossible to believe that you will lose — "

"You can always lose a lawsuit, even the best. If there is a prejudice against me, can I hope they will do us justice? I have seen the judges, and I feel that they are prejudiced against a family which has French connections, particularly now that the relations between the countries are strained. For fifteen months after my father's death no one would have doubted of the success of our suit, but now I do not know what to think. If we lose, all our fortune will be swallowed up. We shall have hardly enough left to live upon!"

"That shall not be!" said I.

"There is everything to fear, Natalis! Not for myself! I am young. I will work! But my mother! Until I have restored her to her position my heart quails at the thought that during those years she will be in misery."

"Good Madame Keller! My sister has told me so much in her praise! You love her dearly?"

"Do I not?"

M. Jean was silent for a moment. Then he resumed: "If it had not been for this lawsuit, Natalis, I should have realized our fortune, and, as my mother has only that one wish, returned to France, which twenty-five years of absence has not made her forget. I would have arranged matters so as to have given her that joy in a year, in a few months perhaps."

"But," asked I, "whether the suit is won or lost, can she not leave Germany?"

"What, Natalis, return to the Picardy she loves without the modest competence to which she is accustomed? How painful that would be to her! I will work, and with all the more courage that it is for her! Shall I succeed? Who can say, particularly amid the troubles I see coming on, when commerce will suffer so much."

To hear M. Jean speak thus gave me such feelings as I did not care to hide. Many times he took me by the hand. I responded to his clasp, and he understood what I felt. What would I not have done to save him and his mother from trouble!

Then he stopped speaking, and gazed with fixed eyes like a man who was regarding the future.

"Natalis!" said he to me in a strange tone, "have you noticed how things arrange themselves at cross-purposes in this world? My mother has become a German by her marriage, and I shall remain a German although I marry a French woman!"

30

This was the only allusion to the project of which Irma had told me in the morning. As M. Jean said no more I did not think it right to say anything. You have to be discreet with people who show friendship to you. When it was convenient for M. Keller to speak to me at length he would find an ear open to listen to him, and a tongue ready to compliment him.

Our walk continued. We talked of one thing and another, and particularly of my affairs. I had to say something about my campaign in America. M. Jean thought that France had acted well in helping the Americans to gain their freedom. He envied the lot of our countrymen, high or low, whom fortune had sent to help the just cause. If he had had the chance he would not have hesitated. He would have volunteered among the soldiers of Comte de Bochambeau. He would have bitten his cartridge at York- town. He would have fought to rescue America from the English domination.

And from the manner in which he spoke, his thrilling voice, and his emphasis which went to my heart, I felt sure that M. Jean would have done his duty. What great deeds would he not have done, and could he not have done! But it is destiny, and we must take it as it comes.

We returned toward Belzingen. The nearest houses were growing white in the sun. Their red roofs, plainly visible among the trees, glowed like flowers amid the foliage. We were about two gunshots off, when M. Jean said to me: "To-night, after supper, my mother and I have a visit to pay."

"May it not bore you!" I answered. "I will remain with my sister."

"No, on the contrary, Natalis, I ask you to come with us."

"As you please."

"They are compatriots of yours — Monsieur and Mademoiselle tie Lauranay, who have lived for some time at Bel- zingen. They will be pleased to see you on account of your coming from their country. And I should like you to make their acquaintance."

31

"Your words are commands," said I.

I understood well enough that M. Jean wished to introduce me further into his family secrets. But, thought I, would not this marriage be an obstacle to his return to France? Would it not be a tie that would attach him and his mother to the country if M. de Lauranay and his daughter had settled in it without hope of return? But I should soon know what to think. A little patience! You must not turn quicker than the mill or you Will grind bad flour.

We had reached the first houses of Belzingen. Already M. Jean had entered the principal street, when I heard the distant sound of a drum.

There was then in Belzingen a regiment of infantry, the Leib regiment, commanded by Colonel von Grawert. I learned later on that this regiment had been in garrison for five or six months. Probably on account of the movement of troops to the westward, it would soon join the bulk of the Prussian army.

A soldier always likes looking at other soldiers, even when they are foreigners. He likes to see what is good and what is bad about them. It is a matter of professional interest to him. From the last button of the gaiters to the plume in the cap, he examines their uniforms and notes the way they march. It is always of interest to him. I stopped accordingly; and so did M. Jean. The drummers were beating one of those marches of continuous rhythm which are of Prussian origin.

Behind them four companies of the Leib regiment kept step. It was not a departure, but merely a military promenade.

M. Jean and I stood by the side of the road to see them pass. The drummers had arrived opposite to us when I felt M. Jean catch hold of me by the arm as if he wished to keep himself from running away.

I looked at him.

"What is the matter?" I asked.

"Nothing."

But M. Jean had first become pale, and now the blood was rising in his cheeks. It looked as though he had been stunned. Then his look became fixed, and it would have been difficult to distract it.

At the head of the leading company, on the left, marched a lieutenant, and, consequently, he was on the side where we stood.

He was one of those German officers whom I had seen so often, and have seen so often since. Rather a good-looking man, fair, and inclined to be sandy, with cold, blue eyes, and dandified swaggering air. In spite of his pretension to elegance you could see that he was a clumsy fellow after all. For my part the fop inspired me with antipathy, even with repulsion.

Doubtless that is what he inspired M. Jean with; perhaps it was more than repulsion. I noticed, too, that the officer did not seem to be animated with the best sentiments toward us. His look was anything but pleasant.

He was only a few paces from us as he passed. And at the moment he passed he made a disdainful gesture with his shoulders. M. Jean's hand clasped mine with a grip of anger. In a moment I felt he might leap on to him; he was restraining himself.

Then the company passed, and the battalion disappeared at a turn in the road.

M. Jean had not said a word. He looked after the soldiers as they disappeared. He seemed to be nailed to the spot. He remained until the sound of the drums ceased to be heard. Then he turned to me and said: "Come, Natalis! let us go to school!" And we went into Mme. Keller's.

CHAPTER VI

I HAD a good master. "Would I do him credit? I did not know. To learn to read at one-and-thirty is not easy. You should have the brain of a child, the soft wax that will take any impression you put upon it; and my brain was as hard as the skull which covered it.

I set resolutely to work, however, and in truth I had to learn quickly. All the vowels were settled in the first lesson. M. Jean showed a patience for which I was grateful. To fix these letters in my memory he made me draw them in pencil ten times, twenty times, a hundred times, one after the other. In this way I learned to write as well as to read. I recommend this method to scholars of my age.

Zeal and attention did not fail him. I would have stuck at my alphabet all night if the servant had not come and told me supper was ready. I went up to my room, which was near my sister's, and I washed my hands and came down.

Supper took us but half an hour. As we were not going to M. de Lauranay's till a little later I asked permission to go outside. This was granted me, and on the steps I gave myself the pleasure of smoking what we Picards call the pipe of tranquillity.

That done I went in. Mme. Keller and her son were ready. Irma having something to do in the house, did not go with us. We started. Mme. Keller asked me for my arm. I offered it, rather clumsily perhaps. No matter! I was proud to feel the excellent lady leaning on me. It was an honor and a pleasure at the same time.

We had not far to walk. M. de Lauranay lived at the upper end of the road. His was a beautiful house, bright in color and attractive in look, with a bed of flowers in front, two large beech-trees at each side, and a large garden behind with shrubbery and lawn. The house showed that the owner was in easy circumstances. And M. de Lauranay was comfortably well off.

Just as we entered, Mme. Keller told me that Mlle, de Lauranay was not M. de Lauranay's daughter, but his granddaughter. I was, therefore, not surprised at their difference in age.

M. de Lauranay was then seventy years old. He was a man of tall stature whom age had not yet bent. His hair was gray rather than white, and it bordered a fine, noble- looking face. His eyes looked at you with a very gentle expression. In his manners you could easily recognize the man of quality. Nothing could be pleasanter than his address.

The "de "in his name unaccompanied by a title showed that he belonged to that class between the nobility and the shop-keeper class, which had not despised manufacture or commerce. If personally he had not been engaged in business his grandfather and father had been. And if he found a fortune ready to his hand we can not blame him for it.

The family of De Lauranay was of Lorraine origin, and Protestant in religion, like that of M. Keller. His ancestors had left France after the revocation of the Edict of Nantes, but not with the intention of remaining abroad. They intended to return to their country as soon as it returned to more liberal ideas. M. de Lauranay lived at Belzingen, in this corner of Prussia, because he had inherited from his uncle certain estates that he could not profitably sell. He would have preferred to sell them and return to Lorraine, but unfortunately no opportunity presented itself. M. Keller, the father, could only get offers at a low price, for money is not plentiful in Germany; and, rather than part with them at a loss, M. de Lauranay thought it best to keep them.

The business relations between M. Keller and M. de Lauranay led to friendship between their families. This had lasted for twenty years. Never had a cloud obscured an intimacy founded on a resemblance of tastes and habits.

M. de Lauranay had lost his wife when he was young; and his son the Kellers hardly knew. He was married in France, and came only once or twice to Belzingen. His father went to see him every year, and thus had the pleasure of passing a few months in France.

The son had a daughter who cost her mother her life, and, much afflicted at the loss, he soon died. His daughter hardly knew him, for she was but five years old when she was left an orphan. Her only relation was her grandfather, who did not fail in his duty.

He sought out the child, brought her back to Germany, and devoted himself entirely to her education. In this he was helped by Mme. Keller, who took a great liking to the child, and treated her as if she had been her mother. That M. de Lauranay was glad to be on terms of friendship with a lady like Mme. Keller I need not say.

My sister Irma, as may be supposed, cordially helped her mistress. Often I know she nursed the little girl on her lap, or got her to sleep in her arms, and that not only with the approbation but with the thanks of her grandfather. To be brief, the little girl became a charming young woman, whom I at the moment looked at with much discretion, for I did not want to embarrass her in any way.

She was born in 1772, and was thus twenty years of age. She was tall for a lady, fair, with dark-blue eyes and a charming face, and a figure full of grace and ease, and not at all like the rest of the feminine population of Belzingen. I admired her straightforward, gentle look, not more serious than it ought to be, and her happy expression. She was the possessor of many gifts as agreeable to herself as to others. She could play the harpsichord very prettily, excusing herself at not being proficient at it, though to a quartermaster like me she seemed to be perfect at it; and she painted beautiful bouquets of flowers on paper screens.

It is not to be wondered at that M. Jean Keller fell in love with this young lady, or that Mlle, de Lauranay took notes of all that was good and amiable in the young man, nor that the families saw with pleasure the growth of the intimacy between the young people. They had, in fact, agreed to let matters take their course. And if the marriage had not taken place it was on account of an excess of delicacy on M. Jean's part — a delicacy which all will appreciate who have their hearts in the right place.

It will not have been forgotten that the position of the Kellers was seriously threatened. Before his marriage M. Jean wished that the lawsuit on which his future depended should come to an end. If he won it, all the better. He would bring Mlle, de Lauranay a fortune. But if he lost the suit he would have nothing. Certainly Mlle. Martha was rich, and would be richer when she lost her grandfather; but M. Jean felt reluctant to share in what she had. And in my opinion the sentiment did him honor.

Circumstances, however, were becoming pressing for him to act in the matter. The marriage was agreeable and suitable to both families; their religion was the same, and they were of the same nationality, at least in the past. If the young couple settled in France, why should not their children become naturalized French subjects? In fact, everything was as it ought to be.

But it was necessary to decide, and without delay, because as things were then an excuse was given for the assiduities of a rival.

Not that M. Jean had cause to be jealous! And how could he be when he had only to say the word and mademoiselle would become his wife!

But it was not jealousy he felt, but a deep and very natural irritation against the young officer we saw with the Leib regiment during our walk in Belzingen.

For some months Lieutenant Frantz yon Grawert had taken notice of Mlle, de Lauranay. Belonging to a family that was rich and influential, he did not doubt for a moment that the De Lauranays would be much honored by his attentions.

And so this Frantz wearied Mlle. Martha with his assiduities. He followed her in the street with such persistency that she hesitated to go out.

M. Jean knew this. More than once he was nearly quarreling with this fop, who kicked up such a dust in the high society of Belzingen; but he had been kept from doing so by the fear of Mlle. Martha's name being mixed up in the affair. When she was his wife, if this officer continued to pursue her he could soon settle him. At present it was best not to notice his attentions.

About three weeks before, however, Mlle, de Lauranay's hand had been asked in marriage on behalf of Lieutenant Frantz. His father, the colonel, had called on M. de Lauranay. There he had told of his fortune, his titles, and the future that awaited his son. He was a brusque man, accustomed to command, tolerating neither hesitation nor refusal — ha fact, a Prussian from his spurs to his plumes.

M. de Lauranay thanked Colonel von Grawert, and expressed himself much honored by his call, but prior arrangements rendered the marriage impossible.

The colonel was politely bowed out, and retired much annoyed at his ill-success. Lieutenant Frantz was very angry. He knew that Jean Keller, a German like himself, was received into M. de Lauranay's house on a footing that was denied to him; and in consequence he cherished a hatred and a desire for revenge that only waited for opportunity.

Urged by jealousy or anger, the young officer continued his attentions; and mademoiselle had decided never to go out either alone, as German custom permitted, or with her grandfather, or with Mme. Keller, or with my sister.

These things I learned after a time, but I thought it better to mention them now.

I could not wish for a better welcome than I received from M. de Lauranay.

"Irma's brother must be a friend of ours," said Mlle. Martha; "and I am glad to shake hands with you."

And, will you believe it? I had nothing to say in reply! If ever I was stupid it was during that day. I was so confused that I said nothing. And the hand was held out to me so gracefully! At last I touched it, but I scarcely pressed it for fear of hurting it. What would you have had? I was only a poor quartermaster!

Then we went into the garden and walked. The conversation put me more at my ease. They spoke of France. M. de Lauranay questioned me as to the events in progress. He seemed to fear that they would give rise to much annoyance to his fellow-countrymen in Germany, and wondered if it would not be better for him to leave Belzingen and return to Lorraine.

"Are you thinking of going?" asked M. Keller.

"I fear we shall be obliged to go, my dear Jean."

"But we should not like to go back alone," added Mlle. — Martha. "When is your leave up, Monsieur Delpierre?"

"In two months," I replied.

"Well, my dear Jean," she continued, "can not Monsieur Delpierre be present at our marriage before he goes?"

"Yes, Martha, yes!"

M. Jean did not know what to answer. His reason and his heart were at variance.

"Mademoiselle," said I, "I shall indeed be happy — "

"My dear Jean," she continued, "can not we give Monsieur Natalis Delpierre this happiness?"

"Yes, dearest Martha," said he, unable to say anything else, although that seemed enough.

And just as we were going away, for it was getting late, Mme. Keller clasped her in her arms and said, with deep emotion: "My daughter, you will be happy! He is worthy of you."

"I know it," said mademoiselle. "Is he not your son?"

We went back to the house. Irma was waiting for us. Mme. Keller told her that all was over except fixing the wedding-day.

Then we went to bed, and if ever I passed an excellent night, notwithstanding the vowels of the alphabet which danced through my dreams, it was this one.

CHAPTER VII

It was late next morning when I awoke. It was quite seven o'clock. I made haste to dress myself — so as to learn my lesson, and get my vowels perfect, ready for the consonants.

As I reached the last steps of the staircase I met Irma.

"I was coming up to wake you," she said.

"Yes. I have been too long abed, and I am late."

"No, Natalis, it is only seven o'clock. But there is some one below asking for you."

"Some one?"

"Yes — a policeman."

A policeman! I do not care for those customers! What did he want with me? My sister did not seem too much at her ease.

At this moment M. Jean appeared.

"It is a policeman," he said. "Take care, Natalis, to say nothing that may get you into trouble."

"It may be that he knows I am a soldier."

"That is not likely! You have come to Belzingen to see your sister, and for nothing else."

And that was the truth, and I resolved to be cautious. I reached the door. There I saw the policeman; a villain in disguise, there could be no doubt, with a body all awry, legs like those of a camp-stool, and a drunkard's face with a shelving throat, as they say.

M. Jean asked him in German what he wanted.

"You have a traveler here who came to Belzingen yesterday."

"Yes. What then?"

"The director of police has given me the order for him to come to the office."

"Well; he will go."

M. Jean explained to me the result of the conversation. It was not an invitation, but an order that I received. I must obey it, therefore.

Spindleshanks took himself off. I liked him better for that. It rather went against me to have to walk through the streets of Belzingen with that catclipole! I was told where the director of the police was to be found.

"What sort of a man is he?" I asked M. Jean.

"Rather a crafty fellow, and you had better mind what you are about with him. His namo is Kalkreuth. He is always trying to annoy us, for he has discovered we take much interest in French matters. We keep him at arins'- length, and he knows it. I should not be surprised if he does not try to implicate us in some rascally affair, so be guarded in your words."

"Will you not come with me?" asked I.

"Kalkreuth did not send for me, and I do not think he would be pleased to see me."

"Can he jabber French at all?"

"He speaks it well. But do not forget, Natalis, to think before you speak, and do not tell him more than is necessary."

"Never fear," said I.

Kalkreutli's house was close by, and I was soon there.

The policeman opened the door, and introduced me into the director's presence.

He greeted me with a smile, I suppose, for his lips opened from one ear to the other. Then in inviting me to sit down he favored me with a gesture which in his estimation was most gracious.

At the same time he ran his finger through a bundle of papers on the table. I reconnoitered my Kalkreuth. He was a fellow of about five feet eight, very long in the chest, skinny, and bony, with huge feet, and a face like parchment, that was always dirty even when it was washed; large mouth, yellow teeth, turn-up nose, wrinkled temples, little, piercing eyes, mere luminous points under thick lids — in fact, a face like a blister. I had been told to distrust him — there was no need for the caution. The distrust came of itself as soon as I found myself in his presence.

When he had finished fiddling with his papers he cocked up his nose, and in very clear French began to question me. But in order that I might have time to think I pretended I had some difficulty in understanding him.

"Your name?" said he.

"Natalis Delpierre."

"Frenchman?"

"Frenchman."

"Your trade?"

"Traveling merchant."

"Traveling merchant? Explain. I do not understand what that means."

"Yes. I go about to fairs and markets to buy and sell things. In fact I travel."

"You have come to Belzingen?"

"Apparently."

"What for?"

"To see my sister, Irma Delpierre, whom I have not seen for thirteen years."

"Your sister is a French woman in Madame Keller's service?"

"Just so."

Then there came a pause in his questions.

"Has your journey no other object?"

"None."

"And when you leave?"

"I shall go back by the road I came."

"And you will do well. When do you think of going away?"

"When I find it convenient to do so. I suppose a stranger can move about Prussia as he pleases?"

"Maybe."

As Kalkreuth said this he gave me a keen look. My answers doubtless were more decided than he liked. But the look was only a flash, there were no signs of thunder as yet.

"Wait a bit!" said I to myself. "This fellow means mischief. I must be on my guard."

Kalkreuth resumed in his sweetest tones.

"How long did you take coming here from France?"

"Nine days."

"And which way did you come?"

"The shortest and the best."

"May I ask you to tell me exactly the way you came?"

"Sir," said I, "why all these questions, if you please?"

"Monsieur Delpierre," said he, dryly, "in Prussia we are accustomed to question strangers who visit us. It is merely a matter of form. You do not intend to object?"

"No! I came from the Dutch frontier, through Brabant, Westphalia, Luxemburg, Saxony — "

"Then you went a long way round?"

"How so?"

"You arrived at Belzingen by the road from Thur- ingia?"

"Yes, from Thuringia."

I saw he knew what he was about. It would not do to contradict myself.

"Can you tell me where you crossed the French frontier?"

"At Tourney."

"That is strange."

"Why is it strange?"

"Because you have been reported as coming from Zerbst."

"That is explained by my not coming here direct."

Evidently I had been watched, and probably by the innkeeper at Ecktvende. It will be remembered that he had seen me arrive when my sister was waiting for me on the road. It was clear enough Kalkreuth wished to get out of me some news from France. More than ever I must be cautious.

He continued: "Then you did not meet with any Germans in the neighborhood of Thionville?"

"No."

"And you know nothing of General Dumouriez?"

"Nothing."

"Nor nothing of the movements of the French troops on the frontier?"

"I know nothing."

Then Kalkreuth's face changed, and his voice became imperious.

"Take care, Monsieur Delpierre," he said.

"Of what?"

"It is not a good time for strangers to travel in Germany, particularly if they are Frenchmen. We do not like them seeing what is taking place here."

"But you would not be sorry to know what is taking place elsewhere! I am not a spy, sir."

"I hope not, for your own sake," said Kalkreuth, in a threatening tone. "I shall keep an eye on you. You are a Frenchman. You have already visited at a Frenchman's house — Monsieur de Lauranay's. You are staying with the Kellers, who keep up correspondence with France. That is enough under present circumstances to make you suspected."

"Was I not free to come to Belzingen?"

"Quite."

"Are Germany and France at war?"

"Not yet. Tell me, Monsieur Delpierre, you seem to have good eyes?"

"Excellent."

"Well, do not use them too much!"

"Why not?"

"Because when you look you see, and when you see you are tempted to tell what you have seen."

"For the second time I tell you I am not a spy."

"And for the second time I say I hope not. If so — "

"If so — what?"

"You will compel me to have you sent back to the frontier, unless — "

46

"Unless what?"

"Unless, in order to spare you the fatigue of the journey, we think it better to give you board and lodging for a more or less extended period."

And so saying, Kalkreuth by a gesture indicated that I might go. This time at the end of his arm there was not an open hand, but a closed one.

Not caring to stay longer than I could help in a police- office, I turned on my heel, a little too much in military style, perhaps. And I am not at all sure that Kalkreuth did not notice it.

I returned to M. Keller's house. But I had been warned. They would not lose sight of me.

M. Jean was waiting for me. I told him in detail what had passed.

"I am not at all surprised," he said "You have not done with the Prussian police. For you as for us, Natalis, I fear there will be trouble in the future."

CHAPTER VIII

The days went by pleasantly enough in walking and study. My young master could testify to my progress. The vowels had been well fixed in my head. We had attacked the consonants. They gave me a good deal of trouble — particularly the last ones. But I got through. Then I came to putting the letters together to form words. It appeared that I had good abilities — for a boy of thirty-one.

We had heard no more from Kalkreuth. I had received no order to present myself at his office. But there was no doubt we were watched, particularly your humble servant, although my way of life gave no occasion for suspicion. I thought I had got off with a warning, and that the director of police would not have the trouble of putting me into lodgings, or escorting me to the frontier.

During the following week M. Jean was away for a day or two. He had to go to Berlin about his lawsuit. At any cost he wanted a decision, for the position was urgent. How would he be received? Would he come back without even having the date fixed for the trial? Would they try to gain time? It was to be feared so.

During M. Jean's absence I was told off, at Irma's suggestion, to keep an eye on the proceedings of Frantz von Grawert. But as Mlle. Martha only went out once, to go to church, she was not met by the lieutenant. Every day he passed M. de Lauranay's house several times, sometimes on foot, swaggering along, and creaking his boots, sometimes cavalcading and caracoling on his horse — a magnificent animal; like his master. But the windows were down, and the door was shut. I leave you to imagine how he fumed. But it showed we had better hurry on the marriage. And it was on account of this that M. Jean had gone for the last time to Berlin. Whatever happened he had decided that the wedding-day should be fixed as soon as he came back to Belzingen.

M. Jean went away on the 18th of June. He could not come back till the 21st. While he was away I worked with ardor. Mme. Keller took her son's place with me; and filled it with a consideration that left nothing to be desired. With what impatience we awaited the return of the absent you can imagine. In fact, matters were pressing. You will see that by what follows, and which I am going to tell you in the light of what I learned later on, without at the time taking much notice of it, for — I confess it willingly — when the pool of politics is stirred, not a drop of it is intelligible to me.

Ever since 1790 the French emigres had taken refuge at Coblenz. In 1791 King Louis XVI. had accepted the constitution, and informed the powers of his acceptance. England, Austria, and Prussia then protested their friendly intentions. But could they be trusted? Would not the emigres persist in urging them to war? They were forming reg-'ments and equipping them. Although their king had ordered them to return to France they had not stopped their preparations. Although the legislative assembly had summoned the electors of Treves, Mayence and the other princes of the empire to disperse the musters on their frontier, yet they were always there ready to lead the invaders.

And then three armies were organized in the east in such a way as to help them.

The Comte de Rochambeau, my old general, took the command of the army of the north, in Flanders. Lafay ette took that of the army of the center at Metz. Luckner took that of the army of Alsace. In all there were 200,000 men, as many sabers as bayonets. "Why should the emigres renounce their projects, and obey the orders of their king when Leopold of Austria was preparing to come to their aid?

Such was the state of affairs in 1791. And in 1792 the state of affairs was as follows: In France, the Jacobins, with Robespierre at their head, had vigorously pronounced against war. The Cordeliers supported them, fearing the rise of a military dictator. On the other hand, the Girondins, through Louvet and Brissot, demanded this war at all cost, so as to force the king to reveal his intentions.

Then it was that there appeared Dumouriez, who had commanded in Vendee and Normandy. He was called to put his military genius and political ability at the service of his country. He accepted and drew up a plan of campaign; a plan at once offensive and defensive. "With him there was no chance of things lying idle.

But up to then Germany had not moved. Her troops did not menace the French frontier, and she even said that nothing would be worse for the interest of Europe. "When things were in this way Leopold of Austria died. What would his successor do? "Would he be a partisan of moderation? No, and a note came forth requiring the re-establishment of the monarchy on the basis of the royal declaration of 1789.

As you may think, France could not submit to such an injunction, which was out of all reason. The effect of the note was considerable throughout the country. Louis XVI. had to propose to the National Assembly to declare war against Francis I. King of Hungary and Bohemia. This was agreed to, and it was resolved to attack him first in his possessions in Belgium.

Then Biron seized on Quievrain, and there was hope that nothing would stop the dash of the French troops when there came a panic at Mons that changed the whole situation. The soldiers raised shouts of treason, and massacred their officers Dillon and Berthois.

When he heard of this disaster, Lafayette stopped his march at Givet.

This happened in the last days of April, before I left Charleville. At this moment, as you see, Germany was not yet at war with France.

On the 13th of June Dumouriez was appointed Minister of War. That we learned at Belzingen, before M. Jean returned from Berlin. It is easy to see that these events would intensify the situation. In fact if Prussia up to then had kept neutral it was to be feared that at any moment she might declare war. They were already talking of 80,000 men on the march to Coblenz.

At the same time a report spread that the command of the old soldiers of Frederick the Great would be given to a general rejoicing in a certain celebrity in Germany, the Duke of Brunswick.

You can understand the effect of this news even before it was confirmed. The passage of the troops was incessant.

I would have given much to see the Leib regiment and Colonel Grawert and his son Frantz depart for the frontier. That would have rid us of these people. Unfortunately the regiment received no order. And so the lieutenant continued to haunt the streets of Belzingen, and particularly the one in front of the closed house of M. de Lauranay.

And for my own part I had something to think about.

I had a regulation leave, it is true, and in a country that had not yet broken with France. But could I forget that I belonged to the Royal Picardy, and my comrades were in garrison at Charleville, close to the frontier?

Assuredly, if we came to blows with the soldiers of Francis of Austria, or Frederick William of Prussia, the Royal Picardy would be in tie first line to get the first round, and I should be desperate at not being there to take my share in it.

I began to be seriously uneasy. But I kept my uneasiness to myself, not wishing to worry Mme. Keller or my sister. But, under the circumstances, the position of a Frenchman was a difficult one. My sister saw that, so far as concerned herself. Of her own free will she would never have separated from Mme. Keller; but what would she do if measures were taken against foreigners? and if Kalkreuth gave us twenty-four hours in which to leave Belzingen?

Our anxieties can therefore be imagined. They were not lessened when we thought of the position of M. de Lauranay. If he was compelled to leave the country, and cross a territory in a state of war, how dangerous the journey would be for both himself and his granddaughter! And where and when was the wedding to take place? Would there be time to celebrate it at Belzingen? In truth we were sure of nothing.

Every day there passed through the town troops on the road to Magdeburg — infantry, cavalry — mostly lancers — their ammunition wagons and carts in hundreds. There was an incessant beating of drums and blaring of trumpets. Frequently there was a halt of a few hours in the principal square. And then what a bustle there was, and what glasses of schnapps and kirschwasser, for the heat was great!

It will be understood that I could not keep myself from going to see, regardless of displeasing M. Kalkreuth. Wherever I heard a trumpet-call or a drum-roll, I was off, if I could get away. I say, if I could get away, for if Mme. Keller was giving me a lesson in reading, nothing in the world would have made me leave her. When the hour for recreation came I slipped out-of-doors, lengthened my stride, struck the route of the troops, followed them to the square, and there I looked at them, although M. Kalkreuth had told me to look at nothing.

If all this activity interested me as a soldier, in my position as a Frenchman I could not but say, "Stop a moment! That looks bad!" It was obvious that hostilities would soon break out.

On the 21st, M. Jean returned from his journey to Berlin. As we had feared, his journey had been futile. The lawsuit remained just as it was. It was impossible to see what would be the end, or when it would come. It was enough to drive us to despair.

From what he had heard, M. Jean reported that any day Prussia might declare war against France.

CHAPTER IX

The next and following days we were all expecting the news. Something would happen within the week at the outside. There were passages of troops through Belzingen on the 21st, 22d, and 23d. A general passed through whom I was told was Count Kaunitz, and he had his staff with him. This mass of soldiers were bound for Coblenz, the emigres were waiting for them. Prussia had joined hands with Austria, and made no secret of the fact that she was marching against France.

The position at Belzingen grew worse from day to day. Evidently it would not improve for the family of M. de Lauranay or my sister Irma when war was declared. To be in Germany under such conditions was to incur great embarrassment — real peril, in fact — and almost anything was to be expected.

I often talked over matters with my sister. The good creature tried in vain to hide her uneasiness. The fear of having to leave Mme. Keller gave her not a moment's rest. To leave the family! Never did she think that the future had such trouble in reserve for her. To go away from those she loved so much, with whom she had thought her whole life would be spent, perhaps never to see them again if events turned out badly, was enough to make her distracted.

"It will be the death of me, Natalis!"

"I understand you, Irma," I replied; "the position is a difficult one, but you must get ready to go. Look here! Can not you get Madame Keller to leave Belzingen now that there is nothing to keep her in this country? I think it would be better to make up your minds to it before things get quite desperate."

"That would be the best, Natalis; but Madame Keller would never consent to leave her son."

"And why should not Monsieur Jean come with us? Why should he stay in Prussia? His business? He could manage that later! This lawsuit which has no end? May he not have to wait months and months before he gets a decision?"

"Probably."

"What makes me most uneasy is this marriage between Monsieur Jean and Mademoiselle Martha! Do they not know what hinderances and delays may happen? If they expel the French from Germany — as is very likely — Monsieur de Lauranay and his granddaughter will have to go in twenty-four hours! And then, what a cruel separation for the young people! But if the marriage is concluded, whether Monsieur Jean takes his wife to France or remains at Belzingen, at least she will stop with him."

"You are right, Natalis."

"If I were in your place, Irma, I would speak to Madame Keller, she can speak to her son, and they can make haste with the marriage. Once it is over, we can let things go."

"Yes," said Irma, "they ought to be married without delay. But the delay will not come from Mademoiselle Martha."

"No! Excellent girl that she is. But then with a husband — a husband like Monsieur Jean — how safe she will be!

Think, Irma, if alone with her grandfather, an old man, she was obliged to leave Belzingen, to cross Germany, all crowded with troops! "What would become of them? You must make haste to get this matter ended, and must not wait until it has become impossible."

"And do you often meet this officer?"

"Every day nearly. It is unlucky that his regiment remains at Belzingen. I should like mademoiselle's marriage kept quiet until after his departure."

"It would be better if it were."

"If this Frantz hears of it, he is almost sure to try something desperate. Monsieur Jean is just the man to quarrel with him, and there — well, I am not easy in my mind."

"Nor am I, Natalis! We must get this marriage over as soon as possible. There are certain formalities to get through, and I am afraid that bad news will interrupt them."

"Then speak to Madame Keller."

"I will, this very day."

Yes, there was need to hurry; may be it was even now too late!

In fact, an event happened which caused Prussia and Austria to hurry on the invasion. This was the outbreak at Paris on the 20th of June, of which the rumor was designedly spread abroad by the agents of the coalition.

On the 20th of June the Tuileries had been invaded. The populace, led by Santerre, had marched past the Legislative Assembly and rushed at the palace of Louis XVI. Gates had been attacked by axes, railings had been forced down, guns bad been hoisted on to the first-floor, everything showed to what violence the outbreak might attain. The king's calmness, coolness, and courage had saved him as well as his wife and two children. But at what price? His consent to wear the bonnet rouge.

Evidently among the partisans of the court and the constitutional party, this attack on the palace was looked upon as a crime. However, the king remained king. They yielded him certain homage. Eations for the dying! But how long would it last? Those most confident in him gave him two months to reign after these threats and insults. And they were not far out, for six weeks later, on the 10th of August, Louis XVI. was driven from the Tuileries, deposed, and imprisoned in the Temple, from which he only came when he lost his head on the place of the Revolution.

If the result of this outbreak was great in Paris, great throughout France, you can easily imagine what a noise it made in foreign countries. At Coblenz there were shouts of grief, and hatred, and vengeance, and you will not be astonished at their echo resounding in the little corner of Prussia in which we found ourselves. It would not take much now to start the emigres on their march with the Imperialists, as they were already called, to support them, and the terrible war to begin.

So they thought at Paris. Energetic measures had been taken to prepare for all eventualities. The organization of the confederates was begun at once. The patriots having decided to hold the king and queen responsible for the invasion that threatened France, the Commission of the Assembly declared that the nation should be in arms, and that it must act for itself without the interference of the government.

And what was done to give enthusiasm to the cause? A solemn declaration was made by the Legislative Assembly: "The country is in danger!"

This we learned a few days after M. Jean's return, and it caused extraordinary excitement.

The news arrived on the 23d, in the morning. Every hour we might hear that Prussia had replied to France by a declaration of war. There was unbounded agitation all over the country. Orderlies, staff officers, went through the town at full gallop. Orders were continually being interchanged between the troops on the march in the west and those coming from the east of Germany. It was said that the Sardinians were going to join the Imperialists, that they were already advancing and threatening the frontier. Unfortunately it was only too true!

These things threw the Kellers and De Lauranays into a state of extreme anxiety. Personally my position became more and more difficult. Every one saw this, and if I did not speak it was because I did not wish to add to the trouble.

In short there was no time to lose. The marriage ought to take place at once.

It was agreed that the 29th should be the day. This delay would be sufficient for the formalities which at that time were very simple. The ceremony would take place at the church before witnesses chosen from friends of the families. I was to be one of the witnesses. What an honor for a quartermaster!

As soon as it was decided preparations were made as secretly as possible. Nothing was said about what was going to take place except to the witnesses whose presence was indispensable. In these days of trouble it was best to avoid attracting attention. Kalkreuth might have put his nose in. And Lieutenant Erantz might be tempted to do something to gratify his vengeance. And these were complications we wished at all cost to avoid.

There was not much time for the preparations. But things were to be very simple, and without any of the entertainments that under less anxious circumstances would have been expected. Not an hour was to be lost. It was not the time to quote the old Picard saying, "There is no need to hurry, for the fair has not yet begun on the bridge."

It had begun on the bridge, and any moment it might get so crowded as to prevent our getting by.

In spite of all our precautions it seemed that the secret was not kept as it should have been. Undoubtedly the neighbors — oh, the neighbors in a provincial town' — were much troubled at what was going on next door. They could not help noticing an unusual running about; and their curiosity was awakened.

Kalkreuth, too, had not ceased to keep his eye on us. No doubt his men had orders to watch us more closely. But what was worse than all was that the news of the marriage reached the ears of Lieutenant von Grawert. My sister learned this from Mme. Keller's servant, who had heard the officers of the Lieb regiment talking about it in the square.

When the lieutenant heard the news he went nearly mad with rage, and told his comrades that the marriage should not take place, and that he would try every means to stop it.

I had hoped that M. Jean would know nothing about this. But unfortunately he was told. He spoke to me about it, and was very angry. I had great difficulty in calming him. He asked me to go to Lieutenant Frantz and demand an explanation, although it was very doubtful if an officer would consent to fight a tradesman as he was.

At last I got him round, and made him understand that by acting in that way he ran the risk of spoiling everything. He gave in, and promised to take no notice of the lieutenant.

The day of the 25th had passed without incident. More than four days to wait. I began to count the hours and minutes. When the ceremony was over we could discuss the serious question of definitely abandoning Belzingen.

But the storm was overhead, and the thunder-clap came in the evening of that day. The terrible news arrived at nine o'clock in the evening.

Prussia had declared war against France.

CHAPTER X

It was the first blow, and a rough one. And perhaps it would be followed by blows that would be rougher. But let us not anticipate, and let us submit to the decrees of Providence, as our cure used to say.

War was thus declared against France, and I, a Frenchman, was in the enemy's country. If the Prussians did not know that I was a soldier, that made matters all the worse for me. My duty was to leave Belzingen by any means, secretly or publicly, and to take my place in the ranks. I had no longer to think of my leave, which had six weeks still to run. The Royal Picardy was at Charleville, only a few leagues from the French frontier. It would take part in the first engagement. I ought to be with it.

But what would become of my sister, of M. de Lauranay, and Mlle. Martha? Would not their nationality cause them serious trouble? The Germans are a rough people, who do not stand upon trifles when their passions are aroused. It was with terror I saw Irma, Mlle. Martha, and her grandfather thrust on the roads of Upper and Lower Saxony, when the Prussian army was there.

There was only one thing to do; to start at the same time as I did, and to return to France with me by the quickest and shortest road. They could trust rne. If M. Jean brought his mother with him and joined us, it seemed to me that we should get through just as well.

But would Mme. Keller and her son do this? It seemed to me simple enough. Was not Mme. Keller a French woman by birth? Was not M. Jean, through her, half a Frenchman? There was no fear of his not being welcomed on the other side of the Rhine when the facts were known. I could not see that he need hesitate. It was the 26th.

The marriage was to take place on the 29 th. There would be no excuse for remaining in Prussia, and the next day we might leave it. It is true we had three days to wait, three centuries rather, in which I gnawed at my bit. Would that these people had been married already!

Yes! Quite so! Was it possible that this marriage that we desired so much, this marriage between a German and a French woman, could be forbidden now that war had been declared? I hardly dared look the position in the face, and I was not alone in thinking seriously about it. At present we avoided alluding to it. We felt it to be a weight that might crush us! What was going to happen? I could not imagine how things would turn out. It did not depend on us to change the order of march!

On the 26th and 27th there was nothing new. Always the troops kept passing through. But it seemed to me the police kept a stricter watch on Mme. Keller's house. I often saw old Spindleshanks, Kalkreuth's man. This constant watching made me uneasy. I was the special object of it; but the Kellers were in the same boat.

It was only too manifest that Mlle. Martha was crying her eyes out. M. Jean kept himself to himself, but he was troubled. I watched him. He became dull and gloomy. He was silent in our presence. He held himself aloof from us. During his visits to M. de Lauranay, it seemed that he was possessed with an idea that he dared not express. On the 28th in the evening we had met at M. de Lauranay's. M. Jean had asked us to go with him, for he wished, so he said, to tell us something he could not keep from us.

. We had begun to talk about one thing and another when the conversation collapsed. Since the declaration of war the line between the French and German race had been definitely drawn, and, as we all understood, M. Jean had been deeply affected by the deplorable complication. Although it was the evening before the wedding, no one spoke about it, and yet if all went well Jean Keller and Mlle. Martha would go to church in the morning, and bind themselves together for life! And yet there was not a word said!

Mlle. Martha rose and went to M. Jean, and said, trying in vain to hide her emotion: "What is the matter?"

"The matter?" said M. Jean in a tone so sad that my heart felt for him.

"Speak," said Martha, "speak, although it may be as painful for us to hear as for you to speak."

M. Jean lifted his head. He felt he was understood before he uttered a word.

No! Never shall I forget the details of this scene if I live to be a hundred!

M. Jean rose and stood before Mlle, de Lauranay and held her hands.

"Martha," said he, "while war remained undeclared between Germany and France I could think of you as my wife. But now my country and yours are about to fight, and when I think of taking you away from your country, of depriving you of your French nationality by marrying you — I dare not do it! I have no right to do it! My life would be a life of remorse! You understand me! I can not do it — "

As if we did not understand him! Poor M. Jean! His words failed him! But was there need for him to speak to be understood?

Mme. Keller, upright in her chair, with her eyes cast down, dared not look at her son. A slight trembling of the lips, a contraction of her fingers, all showed that her heart was ready to break.

M. de Lauranay had dropped his head between his hands. The tears fell from my sister's eyes.

"Those of whom I am one," said M. Jean, "are going to march against France, against the country I love! And who knows how soon I may be called upon to join them?"

He stopped suddenly. His chest heaved, stifled with sobs which he could only repress by superhuman strength, for it is not fitting that a man should weep.

"Speak, Jean," said Mlle, de Lauranay, "while I have strength to listen to you — "

"Martha," he said, "you know that I love you. But you are a French woman, and I have no right to make you a German, an enemy of — "

61

"Jean! And I love you. Nothing that can happen in the future will change my feelings toward you. I love you! and I shall always love you."

"Martha," said M. Jean, falling at her feet. "Dearest Martha, you have heard me talk like this, and to-morrow you would go to church with me! To-morrow you would be my wife, and nothing could separate us! No! It is impossible — !"

"Jean," said M. de Lauranay, "what seems impossible now — "

"May not be so later on!" exclaimed M. Jean. "Yes! This odious war will end! Then, Martha, I can come back to you! Then without remorse I can be your husband!"

And the unhappy man, as he rose, staggered, and nearly fell.

Mlle. Martha stopped him, and in a voice of great tenderness she said: "Jean! I have only one thing to tell you. It does not matter when you come to me, I shall be the same as I am to-day! I understand the feeling which has made you act in this way. Yes! I see that now there is an abyss between us. But I swear before Heaven, that if I am not yours, I shall be no other man's — never!"

And in an irresistible movement Mme. Keller caught her in her arms.

"Martha!" she said, "what my son has done makes him more worthy of you. Later, not in this country, which I wish I had left, but in France, we shall meet again. You will become my daughter, my own child! And it is for my fault you must pardon my son — for being a German!"

Mme. Keller said this in such a tone of despair that M. Jean interrupted her.

"Mother! My mother," he said, "is it for me to reproach you? Should I be so unnatural — "

"Jean," said Mlle. Martha, "your mother is mine."

Mme. Keller opened her arms, and they clasped each other to the heart.

62

If the marriage did not take place before men, owing to circumstances rendering it impossible, at least it took place before God. All that could be done now was to prepare for the departure.

And that evening it was definitely arranged that we should leave Belzingen, Prussia, Germany, where the declaration of war made it impossible for French folks to remain. The lawsuit could not now stop the Kellers. The result could not but be delayed, and they could not wait for it.

It was decided that M. and Mme. de Lauranay should go back with me to France. On this head there was no hesitation, for we were French. Mme. Keller and her son would have to remain in some foreign land while this abominable war lasted. In France they might meet with Prussians, if our country were invaded by the allies. They decided to take refuge in the Low Countries, and await the course of events. We would leave together, and separate when we reached the French frontier.

As our preparations would take a few days, our departure was fixed for the 2nd of July.

CHAPTER XI

After this night there was a sort of relief in the position. A swallowed morsel has no taste, they say. M. Jean and Mlle. Martha were like a married couple obliged to leave each other at any moment. The most dangerous part of the journey, that through Germany, they would travel together; then they would separate until the end of the war. One could then see only the beginning of this long strife against Europe, this long struggle of the Empire during such glorious years, and which was to end to the advantage of the powers of the Coalition.

As for me, I was at last able to rejoin, and I hoped that I should get back in time for Quartermaster Natalis Delpierre to be at his post when the first shot was fired against the soldiers of Prussia and Austria.

The preparations for departure had to be as secret as possible. It was important not to attract attention, especially that of the police. Better to leave Belzingen without anybody knowing of it.

I supposed that nothing would happen to stop us I reckoned without my guest. I say my guest, and really I would not have him come to me for a couple of florins a night; for the guest was Lieutenant Frantz.

I have said that the marriage of Jean Keller and Mlle. Martha de Lauranay had somehow been noised abroad. But it was not known that the night before it had been put off indefinitely. It follows, therefore, that the lieutenat thought the marriage was to be celebrated at once. Now he only had one way of hindering or stopping this marriage, and that was to call out M. Jean and wound him or kill him. But was his hatred keen enough to make him forget his position and his birth, and condescend to fight M. Jean Keller?

There was no doubt if he did he would find some one who was not afraid of him. But in our present circumstances we dreaded the consequences of a duel. I could not help being anxious. The lieutenant, I heard, was as angry as ever, and I feared he would resort to some act of violence.

How unfortunate it was that the Leib regiment had not got its orders to leave Belzingen! The colonel and his son would then be far away, at Coblenz or Magdeburg. I should have been much more comfortable, and so would my sister. Ten times a day I went out to the barracks, to see if they were getting ready for anything, but not the least sign of a move greeted my eyes.

So it was on the 29th; so it was on the 30th. I was happy in reckoning that in twenty-four hours I should be off for the frontier.

I have said we were to travel together. But in order to avoid suspicion it was thought better that Mme. Keller and her son should not start at the same time as we did. They could join us a few leagues from Belzingen. Once out of the Prussian provinces, we should have less to fear from M. Kalkreuth and his dogs.

During this day the lieutenant passed by Mme. Keller's house several times. He even stopped, as if he would like to come inside and arrange matters for himself. Through the blind I could see him without being seen, and note his lips pressed close together, and his hands opening and shutting nervously, and all the signs of intense irritation. In fact, if he had opened the door and asked for M. Jean Keller, I should not have been surprised. Fortunately M. Jean's room looked out of the side of the house, and he saw nothing of this performance.

But what the lieutenant did not do that day he got others to do for him.

About four o'clock a soldier of the Leib regiment came and asked for M. Jean Keller.

He was alone with me at the time in the house, and he read the letter which the soldier handed to him.

What was his anger when he had finished reading it!

The letter was most insolent toward M. Jean and insulting to M. de Lauranay. Yes! Lieutenant von Grawert condescended to insult an old man. At the same time he cast a doubt on the courage of Jean Keller —

and said that if he was not a coward, he could show it in the way he received two comrades who would call on him in the evening.

There could be no doubt in my mind that Lieutenant Frantz knew that M. de Lauranay was preparing to leave Belzingen, and that Jean Keller was going after him, and, sacrificing his pride to his passion, he wished to stop this departure.

In the case of an insult, addressed not only to himself, but to the family of De Lauranay, I expected I should have more difficulty in restraining M. Jean.

"Natalis!" he said, in an angry voice. "I will not go till I have thrashed this scoundrel! I will not go with this stain upon me! It is disgraceful his daring to insult me in all I hold dear. I'll let him see that a demi-Frenchman, as he calls me, is not afraid of a German."

I tried to soothe M. Jean; to point out the consequences of a meeting with the lieutenant. If he wounded him, he might expect such proceedings as would cause us a thousand embarrassments. If he was wounded, how could we go at all?

M. Jean would listen to nothing. I quite understood him. The lieutenant's letter passed all limits. No! It is not allowable to write such things as that! If I could only have taken the matter in my own hands, what satisfaction would it have been! To meet this rascal, provoke him, get him in front of me, point, counterpoint, pistol, anything he liked, and fight him till one of us was brought to the ground. And if it had been M. Lieutenant that fell, I should not have wanted a yard and a half of handkerchief to weep for him in.

"Well, the two comrades of the lieutenant were announced, and we must wait for them.

They came about eight in the evening. Fortunately Mme. Keller was out at M. de Lauranay's. It was better she should know nothing of what was about to happen.

My sister Irma was also out, settling some of the tradesmen's accounts. M. Jean and I were alone.

The officers, two lieutenants, presented themselves with their natural arrogance. That did not astonish me. They wished to make much of the honor done by a noble, an officer, when he consented to fight a tradesman; but M. Jean cut them short by his attitude, and told them at once he was at the orders of M. Frantz von Grawert. It was useless to add fresh insults to those contained in the letter of provocation.

The officers thought it best to put back their boasting in their scabbard.

One of them then remarked that the conditions of the duel should be arranged at once, as time was pressing.

M. Jean answered that he agreed to all the conditions in advance. All he asked was, that no other name should be mixed up in the affair, and that the meeting should be kept as secret as possible. To that the officers made no objection. They had nothing more to do, as M. Jean had left the arrangements to them.

It was the 30th of June. The duel was fixed for nine o'clock next morning. It would take place in a little wood on the left of the road from Belzingen to Magdeburg. There was no difficulty about that.

The men would fight with the saber, and not stop till one of them was unable to continue.

That was agreed. To these propositions M. Jean replied by merely nodding his head.

One of the officers then said — insolence getting the upper hand — that doubtless M. Jean Keller would be at the rendezvous at nine o'clock precisely.

To which M. Jean Keller replied that if M. von Grawert did not keep him waiting, all would be over by a quarter past nine.

At which reply the two officers rose, saluted somewhat cavalierly, and retired.

"You know how to use the saber?" I asked, as soon as they had left.

"Yes, Natalis. But now we must get our seconds. You will be one?"

"At your orders, and proud of the honor! For the other you surely have some friend who will do you this service?"

"I prefer to ask Monsieur de Lauranay, who, I am sure, will not refuse me."

"Certainly not."

"What I wish to avoid above all things is that my mother, Martha, and your sister should be told of this. It is useless to add to their troubles."

"Your mother and Irma will soon come back, Monsieur Jean, and as they will not leave the house till the morning it is impossible for them to find out — "

"So I think, Natalis; and as we have no time to lose, let us go to Monsieur de Lauranay."

"Come on, Monsieur Jean; your honor could;not be in better hands."

Mme. Keller and Irma, accompanied by Mlle, de Lauranay, came in as we were going out. M. Jean said we should be away for about an hour, as he had to see about the horses for the journey.

Mme. Keller and my sister suspected nothing. But Mlle, de Lauranay gave M. Jean an uneasy look. Ten minutes later we found M. de Lauranay alone. We could speak quite freely to him. M. Jean told him what had occurred, and showed him Lieutenant von Grawert's letter.

M. de Lauranay trembled with indignation as he read it. No! Jean could not leave after such an insult! He could reckon on his help.

M. de Lauranay then returned to Mme. Keller's to bring home his daughter.

We then went out together. As we went down the road we noticed Kalkreuth's man in front of us. He gave me a look which I thought a strange one, and as he was coming from Mme. Keller's I had a presentiment that the scoundrel had dealt us some spiteful blow.

Mme. Keller, Mlle. Martha, and my sister were in the little room down-stairs. They seemed in trouble. Had they found out anything?

"Jean," said Mme. Keller. "Here is a letter that Monsieur Kalkreuth's man has just brought."

The letter bore the military seal.

This is what it contained: "All young men under the age of five-and-twenty are hereby called to the colors. The within named, Jean Keller, will join the Leib regiment, at present in garrison at Belzingen. He shall report himself to-morrow, the 7th of July, before eleven o'clock in the morning."

CHAPTER XII

What a blow! A general levy by the Prussian Government! Jean Keller, aged less than twenty-five, liable to the levy! Obliged to join and march with the enemies of France! And no way of escape! Except by deserting, and that was not to be thought of!

And then, to complete the misfortune, he was to serve in this very Leib regiment commanded by Colonel Grawert, the father of Lieutenant Frantz, his rival, now his superior.

What more could happen to overwhelm the Kellers, and all those who were near to them?

Assuredly it was fortunate that the marriage had been postponed. Consider M. Jean married the day before and forced to join his regiment and fight against the countrymen of his wife.

"We were overwhelmed, and we said not a word. Tears fell from the eyes of Mlle. Martha and my sister Irma. Mme. Keller did not weep. She could not. She was as motionless as if she were dead. M. Jean, with his arms crossed, looked round him, steeling himself against fate. I was mad with rage. Do people who do us harm have to pay for it one day or other?

Then M. Jean spoke: "My friends, do not let this change your plans! You were to go to France to-morrow. Go! Do not stop one hour longer in this country than you can help. My mother and I thought of getting into some corner away from Germany. That is not now possible. Natalis, you will take your sister with you."

"Jean, I will remain at Belzingen," said Irma. "I shall not leave your mother."

"You can not — "

"We will stay here, too!" exclaimed Mlle. Martha.

"No!" said Mme. Keller, recovering herself. "You must go. I will remain. I have nothing to fear from the Prussians. Am I not a German?"

And she motioned us toward the door, as if contact with her might be distasteful to us.

"Mother!" exclaimed M. Jean, stepping toward her.

"And what would you have, my son?"

"I would have that you go as well; I would that you go with them to France, to your own country! I am a soldier! My regiment may march any day. You will be alone here, quite alone, and it is not good for you to be so — "

"I will remain, my son. I will remain now you can not go with me."

"And when I leave Belzingen?" continued M. Jean, with his arms round his mother's neck.

"I will go with you."

The reply was made in so resolute a tone that M. Jean was silent. It was not the time to dispute with Mme. Keller. Another time, to-morrow, he would talk to her and bring her to a juster view of the situation. How could a woman accompany an army on the march? To what dangers would she not be exposed? I repeat, it would not have done to contradict her at the moment. She would reflect; she would allow herself to be persuaded.

Then, in an outburst of violent emotion, they separated.

Mme. Keller had not even embraced Mlle. Martha, whom an hour before she had called her daughter.

I went to my room. I did not lie down. How could I sleep? I no longer thought about our departure. And yet it might take place as agreed. I thought only of Jean Keller in the same regiment, and perhaps under the orders of Lieutenant Frantz. Scenes of violence presented themselves to my mind. How could M. Jean put up with such an officer? But he must! He would be a soldier, with not a word to say, not a gesture to make! The terrible Prussian discipline would weigh on him! It was horrible!

"Soldier! No, he is not one yet," I said to myself. "He will not be one till to-morrow, when he takes his place in the ranks. Till then he belongs to himself!"

And that was the way I brought myself to reason — to unreason, rather!

"Yes," I repeated to myself, "to-morrow at eleven o'clock when he joins his regiment he will be a soldier! Till then he has the right to fight this Frantz. And he will kill him, he must kill him, or later on the lieutenant will have only too many occasions to be revenged on him."

What a night I passed! Never do I wish my enemy a worse one!

About three o'clock I had thrown myself on my bed, dressed as I was. I got up at five o'clock, and went quietly to M. Jean's door.

He was up. I held my breath. I listened.

I heard him writing. Doubtless some last arrangements, in the event of the encounter being fatal. Sometimes he walked about once or twice, then he sat down, and the pen resumed its scratching on the paper. There was no other sound in the house.

I did not wish to trouble him. I returned to my room, and at six o'clock I went down into the street.

The news of the levy had got abroad. It produced an extraordinary effect. The measure affected nearly all the young men in the town, and from what I saw it was received with general displeasure. It was a hard measure, in fact, for no one was prepared for it. No one expected it. In a few hours it was necessary to be off, knapsack on back, musket on shoulder.

I did sentry-go before our house. It had been agreed that M. Jean and I should call on M. de Lauranay about eight o'clock, and bring him to the rendezvous. If M. de Lauranay had come to us suspicion would have been aroused.

I waited till half past seven; M. Jean had not yet come down.

Mme. Keller had not appeared in the lower room.

At this moment Irma found me.

"What is Monsieur Jean doing?" asked I.

"I do not know," she replied. "He has not gone out. Perhaps you had better — "

"It is useless, Irma, I heard him moving about in his room."

And then we talked, not of the duel — my sister knew nothing about that — but of the serious state of affairs now this levy had been made.

Irma was in despair, and to separate from her mistress under such circumstances was heart-breaking.

We heard a noise in the upper room. My sister went out for a moment, and came back to tell me that M. Jean was with his mother.

I thought he had gone to kiss her, as was his custom every morning. In his mind it might be a last adieu, a last kiss he was giving her.

About eight o'clock they came down-stairs. M. Jean came to the doorstep.

Irma was just leaving me.

M. Jean shook hands with me.

"Monsieur Jean," I said, "it is eight o'clock, and we must go."

He gave me a nod of the head, as though it cost him too much to speak.

It was time to go to M. de Lauranay. We had gone about three hundred yards up the street when a soldier of the Leib regiment stopped in front of us.

"You are Jean Keller?" he said.

"Yes."

"That is for you."

And he presented a letter.

"Who sent you?" I asked.

"Lieutenant von Melhis."

It was one of the seconds of Lieutenant Frantz. A shudder passed through me. M. Jean opened the letter.

This is what he read:

"Owing to circumstances that have just occurred, a duel is now impossible between Lieutenant Frantz Grawert and Private Jean Keller.

"B. G. Yon Melhis."

My blood boiled within me! An officer could not fight a private! Be it so! But private Jean Keller was not! He belonged to himself for some hours yet!

It seemed to me that a French officer would not have acted like that! He would have given satisfaction to a man he had mortally insulted! He would have come on the ground —

There I stop! I might say too much! And besides, on reflection, was the duel possible?

M. Jean tore up the letter and with a gesture of scorn threw it on the ground, and only these words escaped him: "The scoundrel!"

Then he gave me a sign to follow him, and we returned to the house.

I was so choked with anger that I had to stay outside. I rambled off without knowing where I was going. My brain was upset at thinking of the future. Suddenly it occurred to me that I ought to go and tell M. de Lauranay that the duel would not take place.

It will be believed that I had no notion of the time, for when it seemed I had just left M. Jean, it was about ten o'clock when I found myself again before Mme. Keller's house.

M. and Mlle, de Lauranay were there. M. Jean was preparing to leave them.

I pass over the scene which followed. I have no pen that could describe it in detail. I will content myself with saying that Mme. Keller was worthy of herself, and gave her son no example of feebleness. And on his side M. Jean was sufficiently master of himself not to give way in the presence of his mother and M. de Lauranay.

At the moment of separation Mlle. Martha and he threw themselves for the last time into Mme. Keller's arms.

Then the door of the house closed.

M. Jean had gone! He was a Prussian soldier!

That very evening the Leib regiment received orders to march to Borna, a few leagues from Belzingen, almost on the frontier of the Potsdam district.

In spite of all the reasons M. de Lauranay could advance, in spite of all we could do, Mme. Keller persisted in her idea of following her son. The regiment was going to Boma, she would go to Borna. M. Jean had been unable to shake her resolve.

As for us, our departure must take place next day. What an affecting scene I expected when my sister bade farewell to Mme. Keller! Irma would have remained to accompany her mistress wherever she went. And I — I would hardly have the strength to bring her away with me! Mme. Keller would refuse — my sister would submit.

In the afternoon our preparations were complete. And then everything was upset!

About five o'clock M. de Lauranay received a visit from .Kalkreuth in person.

The director of police informed him that his plans of departure were known, and that he was under the necessity of ordering him to suspend them — for the present at all events. He must wait for the measures government intended to take with regard to French subjects residing in Prussia. He could not grant him passports; and the journey was consequently impossible.

As to Natalis Delpierre, it was another matter! Quite another matter! It seemed that Irma's brother had been denounced as a spy, and Kalkreuth was only too delighted to treat him accordingly. After all, perhaps, they had learned he belonged to the Royal Picardy? For the success of the Imperialists it was doubtless important that there should be one soldier less in the enemy's army!

And so, that very day, I saw myself arrested in spite of the supplications of my sister and Mme. Keller, and then taken by stages to Potsdam, where I was imprisoned in the citadel.

The rage I was in I need not describe! Separated from all those I cherished, unable to escape to regain my post at the moment when the first shots were to be exchanged.

They did not interrogate me, they put me away secretly. I could not communicate with anybody, for six weeks I had no news from outside. But the story of my imprisonment would take me away too far. My friends at Grattepanche would rather that I stuck to the bill of fare. Let it be enough for me to say that the time appeared long, and that the hours rolled by as slowly as the smoke in May. But I was lucky in not being tried, for my case was clear, said Kalkreuth, and I might remain a prisoner till the end of the campaign.

But I did not. A month and a half afterward, on the 15 th of August, the commandant of the citadel gave me my liberty; and they took me back to Belzingen without having had the kindness to tell me for what I had been arrested. That I was happy to see Mme. Keller, my sister, and M. and Mlle, de Lauranay, who had not left Belzingen, I need not say.

As the Leib regiment had not yet gone beyond Borna, Mme. Keller had remained at Belzingen. M. Jean wrote sometimes; as often as he could, no doubt. And in spite of the reserve in his letters, we could feel all that was horrible in his position.

But if they had given me my liberty, they had not allowed me to remain in Prussia. A decree had been issued by the government, expelling the French from their territory. We had twenty-four hours in which to leave Belzingen, and twenty days in which to clear out of Germany.

A fortnight before there had appeared Brunswick's manifesto threatening France with invasion from the coalized powers.

CHAPTER XIII

There was not a day to lose. We had about a hundred and fifty leagues to travel to reach the French frontier — one hundred and fifty leagues through an enemy's country, along roads blocked by regiments on the march, cavalry and infantry, to say nothing of the stragglers that always follow an army in the field. Although we might be sure of the means of transport, we might break down on the road. If our means of transport failed, we should have to go on foot.

Could we reckon on finding inns at the different stages? Evidently not. I alone, long accustomed to privations, marches, and outwalking the strongest walkers, had no fear I should get through in the end. But with M. de Lauranay, an old man of seventy, and two women, Mlle. Martha and my sister, it did not do to expect the impossible. But I would do my best to take them safe and sound to France, and I knew that all would do their best.

As I have said, we had no time to lose. And the police were on our heels. Twenty-four hours to leave Belzingen, twenty days to evacuate the German territory, which would be enough if we were not stopped on the road. The passports Kalkreuth would give us that evening would only be available for that period. The delay over, we might be stopped and detained until the end of the war. The passports would give us an itinerary we were forbidden to depart from, and we would have to get them examined in the towns or villages indicated as halting-places.

It was probable that events would follow each other with extreme rapidity. Perhaps the bullet rain had even now begun on the frontier.

To the Duke of Brunswick's manifesto, the nation, by the mouth of its deputies, had replied: "The country is in danger."

On the 16th of August we were ready at an early hour. All our arrangements had been made. M. de Lauranay's house was to be left in charge of an old domestic, a Swiss by birth, who had been in his service for years, and on whose faithfulness he could depend. Mme.

Keller's house would remain, until it was disposed of, in charge of the servant, who was of Prussian nationality.

In the morning we ascertained that the Leib regiment had just left Borna on the way to Magdeburg.

M. de Lauranay, Mlle. Martha, my sister, and I made another attempt to persuade Mme. Keller to come with us.

"No, my friends," she said; "say no more about it. To-day I will take the road to Magdeburg. I have a presentiment of some great misfortune, and I will be there."

We saw that all our efforts would be in vain, and that Mme. Keller would not yield in her resolution. All we could do was to bid her good-bye, and let her know the towns and villages through which the police required us to go.

Our arrangements were as follows: M. de Lauranay possessed an old mail berline which seemed to me well adapted for our jnurney of one hundred and fifty leagues. In ordinary times it is easy to travel with the relays of horses at the stages on the roads. But in war time, as the horses were requisitioned from all parts for the service of the army, in the transport of ammunition and supplies, it would not have been wise to trust to the relays. In order to avoid any inconvenience, we decided to proceed differently. I was asked by M. de Lauranay to get two good horses, regardless of cost; and as I knew what I was about in such matters, I did very well. I found two, who though rather heavy, perhaps, had plenty of staying power. Then thinking that I should have to dispense with postilions, I volunteered for the duty, and it was naturally accepted. And a Royal Picardy did not want showing how to manage a team!

On the 16th of August, at eight o'clock, everything was ready. I had only to get into the saddle. For arms we had a pair of horse-pistols, with which we could keep marauders at a respectful distance; and we had enough provisions to last us for the first few days. It had been arranged that M. and Mlle, de Lauranay should occupy the back seat of the berline, and that my sister should take the front, facing mademoiselle. I, in a substantial suit, and with a thick wagoner's frock in addition, could face the weather.

The last farewells were said. We embraced Mme. Keller, wondering if we should see her again.

The weather was fine, but in the middle of the day it would probably be very warm. Between now and two o'clock I intended to give the horses a rest, an indispensable rest if we were to travel far.

At last we were off. I began to whistle to cheer up my team, and I rent the air with the cracking of my whip. We got clear of Belzingen without being hindered much by the troops on march to Coblenz. From Belzingen to Borna is about a couple of leagues, and we got there in an hour. There the Leib regiment had been in garrison for some weeks, and from there it had gone to Magdeburg, where Mme. Keller was to reach it.

Mlle. Martha betrayed considerable emotion as we drove through the streets. She pictured to herself M. Jean, under the orders of Lieutenant Frantz, marching along the road which we were obliged to leave on our way to the south-west.

I did not stop at Borna. I intended to keep on four leagues further to the present frontier of the province of Brandenburg. But at this time, according to the old divisions of the German territory, we were in Upper Saxony.

Noon came when we reached this point of the frontier. A few detachments of cavalry were there in bivouac. An isolated inn stood by the road-side. There I could give my horses a meal, and there we stopped for three long hours. On this, the first day of our journey, I considered it prudent to work the horses so as they should not break down at the beginning.

We had to get our passports examined here. As we were French, we of course came in for a few suspicious looks. But that did not matter!

We were all in order. And as they were driving us out of Germany, and as we had to evacuate the territory with as little delay as possible, there was uo reason for stopping us.

Our intention was to pass the night at Zerbst. Only under exceptional circumstances were we to travel during the night. The roads did not seem safe enough for us to risk adventure in the dark. There were too many ugly customers about. In these northern parts the nights in August are not long. The sun rises before three o'clock in the morning, and does not set much before nine. Our halt would thus be only for a few hours — just time enough to give us all a rest. When it became necessary to make an effort, we could do so.

From the frontier, where the berline stopped at noon, to Zerbst is not more than eight leagues. We could do that between three in the afternoon and eight in the evening. And I saw that we might reckon on a good many delays.

This day we had a little difference with a sort of horse recruiter, a long skinny fellow, bragging like a jockey, who tried to requisition our team. It was, he said, for the service of the state. I fancy the state meant the same to him as it did to Louis XIV. and that he wanted it for himself.

But I stopped him at last! He had to give in to our passports and the signature of the director of police; but we lost quite an hour before he would leave us.

We then found ourselves on the territory since formed into the principality of Anhalt. The roads were less crowded now, because the main mass of the Prussian army had inclined off to the north toward Magdeburg.

We met with no difficulty in reaching Zerbst — a sort of village of little importance, with hardly anything to be got in it when we arrived, about nine o'clock. It was obvious that the thieves had been through it, and that they did not at all object to living on the country. We did not want much beyond quarters for the night. But these quarters, among houses prudently shut, we had some difficulty in obtaining. I thought we should have to stay in the berline. We might do that, but how about the horses? Did they not want forage and litter? I thought of them before everything, and I trembled at the thought of their failing us.

I therefore suggested that we should go on to Acken, for instance, three leagues and a half from Zerbst, to the south-west. We could get there before midnight, and start at ten next morning, so as to give the horses a rest. M. de Lauranay told me we should have to cross the Elbe before we reached Acken, and that we should have to go over in a boat, and that it was better to cross during daylight. He was right. We had to cross the Elbe before we got to Acken, and then we might meet with difficulty.

I ought to say that M. de Lauranay knew the road well. For many years during his son's life-time he had traveled between Belzingen and the French frontier. I had only been along the road once, so that he was the best guide, and it was wise to defer to him.

So, purse in hand, we again tried to find quarters at Zerbst for ourselves and horses; and at last we were successful, and we also found something to eat, so as to make the reserves in the berline go further. And so we passed the night at Zerbst more comfortably than we expected.

CHAPTER XIV

Just before we reached Zerbst our berline had entered the territory which forms the principality of Anhalt and its three duchies. Next day we were to traverse it from north to south, so as to reach the little town of Acken. This brought us into Saxony, into the district of Magdeburg. Then Anhalt appeared again, as we headed toward Berns- burg, the capital of the duchy of the same name. Thence, for a third time, we entered Saxon territory, and crossed through Merseburg. Such in these days was the Germanic Confederation, with its hundreds of small states that the Ogre of Petit Poucet was to clear away at one swoop.

As you of course have guessed, I learned all this from M. de Lauranay. He showed me his map, and with his finger pointed out the position of the provinces and chief towns and rivers. I had not been through a course of geography in the regiment. And, again, if I had only known how to read!

Ah! my poor alphabet, suddenly interrupted just as I had begun to put the vowels and consonants together! And my good professor, M. Jean, now with knapsack on back, captured in this levy! But we must not dwell on these things, we must get on our road.

Since the evening the weather had been warm, stormy, dull, with little bits of blue among the clouds, not big enough, as they say, to make a gendarme's breeches. I pushed on the horses, for it was important to reach Berns- burg before nightfall — and that meant a dozen leagues, which was not impossible, if the weather held up and we met with no obstacle.

But the Elbe barred the way, and I feared we should be kept there longer than I wanted.

Leaving Zerbst at six o'clock, we were on the right bank of the Elbe two hours afterward. It is rather a fine river of good breadth, and bordered with high banks and thousands upon thousands of reeds.

Fortune favored us. The ferry-boat was on our side, and as M. de Lauranay spared neither florins nor kreutzers, we did not have to wait long. In a quarter of an hour berline and horses were afloat.

The passage was effected without accident. If we were to be treated in the same way at every river we came to, we should not have much to complain of.

We then reached the small town of Acken, through which we went without stopping, on the road to Bernsburg.

I took the team along at top speed. The roads were not as good then as they are to-day. Mere ribbons traced on uneven ground, made more by the wheels of carts than the hands of man. In the rainy season they would have been impracticable, and in summer they left much to be wished for.

We kept on all the morning without a check. About noon — fortunately during our halt — we were passed by a regiment of pandours on the march. This was the first time I had seen these Austrian cavalry. They passed at full gallop. There was an enormous cloud of dust that rose to the sky, and in the whirlwind were the red reflections of their cloaks and the black spot of the sheepskin cap worn by these savages.

We had turned off the road, and were resting by the side of a small clump of beeches in which I had put the carriage. They did not see us. With such friends there is no knowing what might not happen; our horses might have taken the fancy of the pandours, and our berline that of the officers! Most certainly if we had been on the road they would not have waited for us to stand aside for them; they would simply have swept us away.

About four o'clock I pointed out to M. de Lauranay some high ground ahead, about a league away to the west.

"That is the castle of Bernsburg," he replied.

The castle is on the summit of a hill, and can be seen from a great distance.

I urged on the horses. Half an hour afterward we were in Bernsburg, and there our papers were verified. Then, tired out by the heat of the stormy day, we crossed the Saale in a boat and entered Alstleben about ten o'clock. The night was fine — we were lodged in a fairly comfortable hotel, where we found no Prussian officers; so that our peace was not troubled, and we left at ten o'clock precisely next morning.

I shall not stop to give you the details of all the towns, villages, and hamlets we passed through. We did not see much of them. We were not traveling for pleasure, but were being expelled from a country we left without regret. The important point is that nothing happened to hinder us, and that we made good progress.

On the 18th, at noon, we were at Hettstadt. We had had to cross the Wipper, which in our regiment we called the Viper, not far from the copper mines. At three o'clock we reached Leimbach, at the junction of the Wipper and the Thalbach — another pleasant name for the wits of the Royal Picardy. Having passed Mansfeld, with its high hill, which a ray of sunshine was caressing in a shower of rain, and then Sangerhausen on the Gena, our way lay across a country rich in mines, with the Hartz Mountains on the horizon, and at the close of the day we had reached Artern on the Unstrut.

It had been a very tiring day — nearly fifteen leagues without a stoppage. I had to look well after my horses, and get them a good feed when they arrived, and good litter for the night. That cost something. M. de Lauranay did not, however, mind a few extra kreutzers, and he was right.

We were off next morning at eight o'clock, after a few difficulties with the innkeeper. I know that there is no bad without a worse, but I will back the proprietor of the hotel at Artern as one of the most unscrupulous fleecers of the German Empire.

This day the weather was detestable. There was a heavy storm. The lightning blinded us. Violent peals of thunder frightened the horses, and we were soaked in a pouring rain — one of those rains that rain parsons, as we say in our country.

The next day, the 19th of August, was better. The country was bathed in dew, beneath the breath of the first breeze of the morning. There was no rain. A stormy sky and overpowering heat. The ground was hilly. My horses were tiring. Soon I saw I should have to give them a twenty-four hours' rest. But before that I hoped to reach Gotha.

The road crossed the fairly well-tilled lands around Heldmungen, on the Schmuke, where we halted. "We had not been much bothered during the four days we had left Belzingen, and I thought to myself: "If we had been able to travel together, we might have squeezed Mme. Keller and her son into the berline!"

Our road took us through Erfurth, one of the three districts of the province of Saxony. The roads were good, and our progress was rapid. I should have taken my horses along better if it had not been for an accident to one of the wheels, which we could not get repaired at Weissensee. At Tennstedt we had it taken in hand by a clumsy smith, and it worried me for the rest of the journey.

The stage was a long one to-day, but we were sustained by the hope of reaching Gotha. There we could rest — providing we got comfortable quarters. For me it did not matter much. Strongly built as I was, I could stand much worse treatment than I had had. But M. and Mlle, de Lauranay, although they did not complain, looked quite tired out already. My sister Irma was not so bad. But all of them were very sorrowful.

From five o'clock to nine in the evening we completed eight leagues, having passed Schambach, and left the territory of Saxony for that of Saxe-Coburg. At eleven we reached Gotha. Here we had decided to wait for a day. Our horses had well earned a night and day's rest. I had certainly been lucky when I chose them. There is nothing like knowing what you are buying, and being able to pay the price.

I said we reached Gotha at eleven o'clock. We were delayed a little by the formalities at the gate of the town. If our papers had not been in order we should have been stopped. Both the military officials and the civil officials were as strict as they could be. It was fortunate that the Prussian Government in expelling us had given us the means of obeying. I concluded that if we had tried our first plan of leaving before M. Jean's call to the regiment, Kalkreuth would not have given us our passports, and we should never have reached the frontier. So we had to thank Heaven first of all, and then his Majesty Frederick William for helping us on our journey. It is useless to go to the Cross before the time. That is one of our Picard proverbs, and it is worth a good many others.

There are some good hotels at Gotha. At the Prussian Arms I found four very acceptable rooms, and a stable for two horses. Although I regretted the delay, yet I felt I must resign myself to it. Of the twenty days allowed us for our journey, we had only occupied four, and we had done a third of the distance. If we could keep up at that rate, we should reach the French frontier in the time allowed. I only asked one thing, and that was that the Royal Picardy did not get under fire until I got back.

In the morning, about eight o'clock, I went down to the parlor of the hotel, where my sister joined me.

"How are Monsieur and Mademoiselle de Lauranay?' I asked.

"They have not yet left their rooms," said Irma, "and we must not disturb them till breakfast."

"That is understood, Irma. And where are you going?"

"Nowhere now. But in the afternoon I am going shopping, to make up our stock of provisions. Will you come with me?"

"Willingly. I will be ready. Meanwhile I will go and stroll about the streets."

And off I went in search of adventure.

What shall I tell you of Gotha? I did not see anything very grand. There were many troops — infantry, artillery, cavalry, and commissariat. I heard a good deal of bell-ringing, and saw some guard-relieving. At the thought that all these soldiers were marching against France, my heart was sore. What misery to think that the soil of my country was perhaps to be invaded by these strangers! How many of my comrades would die in defending it! Yes! I ought to be with them to fight at my post. Quartermaster Delpierre was not one of those tin-plates that dread the fire.

In returning I passed many churches whose steeples pointed into the mist. Round them I met with a great number of soldiers. The place seemed nothing but an enormous barracks.

I got back at eleven, having taken the precaution to have our passports examined as we had been ordered. M. de Lauranay was still in his room with Mlle. Martha. The poor girl had not the heart to go out; and that was intelligible. What would she have seen if she had? Nothing but what would have reminded her of M. Jean! Where was he then? Had Mme. Keller been able to come up with him, or at least to follow the regiment from halt to halt? How was she traveling? What could she do in the event of the misfortunes she anticipated? And M. Jean, a Prussian soldier marching against the country he loved, which he would have been happy to have the right to defend, for which he would willingly have shed his blood!

Naturally we were down-hearted. M. de Lauranay had his lunch in his room. The German officers came to the Prussian Arms for their meals, and it was better to avoid meeting them.

After lunch M. and Mlle, de Lauranay remained at the hotel with my sister. I went out to see that the horses wanted for nothing. The innkeeper accompanied me to the stables. I saw that he wanted to talk with me about our journey, and matters that were no business of his. But I was prepared for him, and he did not get much out of me.

At three o'clock my sister and I went out shopping. As Irma spoke German we could get on all right in the streets and shops. All the same they could see easily enough that we were French, and that might not improve their reception of us.

Between three and five o'clock we went to several places, and, in short, I saw all the chief streets of Gotha.

I should like to have heard news of what was happening in France, and I told Irma to keep her ears open to what was being said in the streets and shops. We did not even hesitate to get near such groups as were talking with much animation, in order to hear what they were talking about — which was not very prudent on my part. The little we learned was not very gratifying to a Frenchman; but better have bad news than none at all.

I noticed several placards on the walls. Most of them were announcements of the movements of troops, or tenders for army supplies. Now and then my sister stopped and read the first lines.

One of these notices at length specially attracted my attention. It was written in heavy black characters on yellow paper. I can see it now stuck up against a shed at the corner of a cobbler's stall.

"Look," said I to Irma; "look at that notice! Are those figures at the top?"

My sister approached the stall and began to read: What a cry she gave! Fortunately we were alone. No one heard her.

And this is what the notice said: "One thousand florins reward to any one giving up Jean Keller of Belzingen, a soldier sentenced to death for having struck an officer of the Leib regiment on the march to Magdeburg."

CHAPTER XV

How we got back to the Prussian Arms, and what we said by the way I have in vain tried to remember. Perhaps we did not interchange a word! The trouble in which we were might have been noticed. It would not have taken much to have brought us before the authorities. We might have been questioned, arrested perhaps, if they found by what ties we were bound to the Kellers!

We regained our rooms without running against anybody. My sister and I had a talk together before seeing M. and Mlle, de Lauranay. We wished to agree what had best be done.

There we sat, looking at each other, without daring to say a word.

"Poor fellow! Poor fellow! What has he done?" exclaimed my sister.

"What has he done?" said I. "He has done what I should have done in his place! He has been treated badly and insulted by this Frantz! He has struck him, as was sure to happen sooner or later! I should have done the same!"

"My poor Jean! my poor Jean!" murmured my sister, as the tears rolled down her cheeks.

"Irma," said I, "courage! It was necessary!"

"Sentenced to death!"

"Not so fast! He has run away! At present he is out of their reach, and wherever he may be, he must be better off than in the regiment with the Grawerts!"

"And the thousand florins they promise to any one who will give him up, Natalis!"

"The thousand florins are not in anybody's pocket at present, Irma, and probably no one will ever get them."

"And how can he escape? The notice is up in all the towns and villages. How many low fellows there must be who would like nothing better than to find him!"

"Do not give way so, Irma," I replied. "Nothing as yet is lost! There are many muskets pointing at the man — "

"Natalis! Natalis!"

"But they may miss fire! That is clear! Do not give way, I tell you! Monsieur Jean has escaped and got away into the country. He is alive, and he is not the man to let them catch him. He will be safe!"

I must say candidly that when I said this it was not only with the idea of giving my sister hope. I believed it myself. Evidently M. Jean's greatest difficulty was to escape, and if he had succeeded in that, it did not seem easy to get hold of him again, although the bills offered a reward of a thousand florins. No! I did not despair, although my sister would listen to nothing.

"And Madame Keller?" she said.

Yes! What had become of Mme. Keller? Had she been able to reach her son? Did she know what had happened? Was she with M. Jean in his flight?

"Poor woman! Poor mother!" repeated my sister. "If she reached the regiment at Magdeburg she must have heard of it! She knows her son is sentenced to death!"

"Irma," said I, "be calm! If they were to hear you! You know Madame Keller is a woman of energy; perhaps Monsieur Jean has returned to her!"

This may seem surprising; but, I repeat, I said what I thought was true. It is not in my nature to abandon myself to despair.

"And Martha?" said my sister.

"My advice is to say nothing about it to them. If we speak, they may lose courage. The journey is still a long one, and Mademoiselle Martha wants all her strength of mind. If she learns what has happened — that Monsieur Jean is condemned to death, that he is in flight, that a price is on bis head, she will be half dead! She will refuse to follow us — "

"Yes, you are right, Natalis! Shall we keep it secret from Monsieur de Lauranay?"

"Just as much, Irma. To tell him would do no good. Ah! if it were only possible for us to get away in search of Madame Keller and her son! We might then tell Monsieur de Lauranay everything. But our days are numbered. We are forbidden to remain in this country. We should soon be arrested, and I do not see how that could benefit Monsieur Jean. Come, Irma, be reasonable. Above all, take care that mademoiselle does not notice that you have been crying!"

"And if they go out, Natalis, can they not read that bill and learn — "

"It is not likely, Irma, that they will go out at night if they did not go out during the day. And if they do, it is not easy to read a bill like that in the dark. We need not fear that they will find anything out. So take care of yourself, and be strong."

"I will, Natalis! I feel that you are right! Yes! I will take care. They will see nothing; but when I am alone — "

"When you are alone, you can cry, Irma, for it is all very sad; cry, but be silent! Those are your orders!"

After supper, during which I talked about everything, so as to attract attention to myself and relieve my sister, M. and Mlle, de Lauranay went back to their rooms as I thought they would. After a visit to the stable I went and arranged with them to rise early in the morning. I intended to start at five o'clock sharp, for our road for the day was to be a long one, and a tiring one, and through a mountainous country.

We went to bed. For my part I hardly slept at all. I thought of all that had happened. The confidence I felt when endeavoring to keep up my sister's spirits seemed to be leaving me now. Things might turn out badly. Jean Keller betrayed — handed over. Is it not always thus when you are half asleep?

At five o'clock I was up, and had awakened my people and put-to my horses. I was in a hurry to leave Gotha.

At six o'clock they were all in the berline, I had started my well-rested horses, and was off on my first four leagues. We had reached the mountains of Thuringia.

We had now a difficult journey before us, and a good deal of management was required. It was not that the mountains were very high. They are not Pyrenees, nor are they Alps. But the country is not an easy one for driving through, and I had to be as careful of the carriage as of the horses. There were then hardly any proper roads. There were defiles, often very narrow ones, that we had to make our way through, not without danger; wooded gorges, with thick forests of oaks, firs, beeches, and larches; frequent windings, tortuous footpaths, where the berline could only just get by, with a cliff on one side and a precipice on the other, and a torrent growling below.

From time to time I had to dismount and lead the horses. M. de Lauranay, his granddaughter, and my sister occasionally got out and walked when the ascent was difficult. Often we had to halt to take breath. How I congratulated myself that I had said nothing about M. Jean! If my sister despaired in spite of my reasoning with her, what would have been the despair of Mlle. Martha and her grandfather?

This day, the 21st of August, we did not do five leagues in a straight line — for the road made a thousand curves, and at times seemed to be taking us back again. We should have had a guide, you say? But whom could we trust? Frenchmen at the mercy of a German when war had been declared! No, better trust to ourselves to get out of our difficulties! Besides, M. de Lauranay had trav-

eled through Thuringia so often that he knew the road well. The most difficult part was through the forests. There we had often to trust to the sun, who, not being of German origin, did not lead us astray.

About eight o'clock in the evening the berline stopped at the skirt of a birch wood on the flank of a high chain of mountains. It would have been imprudent to venture further during the night. There was no inn, not even a woodman's hut. We would have to sleep in the berline, I — or under the trees of the forest. We supped on the provisions in our boxes. I had unharnessed the horses. As grass was abundant at the foot of the hill, I left them to graze at liberty, my intention being to watch over them during the night.

I persuaded M. de Lauranay, Mlle Martha, and my sister to resume their places in the berline, where they would at least be under shelter. A slight raiu was falling, a cold drizzle, for we were now at a considerable elevation. i M. de Lauranay offered to pass the night with me. I refused. Such watches are not good for a man of his age. I would rather spend it alone. Wrapped in my warm frock, with the branches of the trees over my head, I should have nothing to complain of. I had done the same before in the prairies of America, where the winter is worse than in any other climate.

Everything went as well as could be wished. Our tranquillity was not disturbed. The berline was as good as many of the rooms in the hotels. With the windows closed there was no damp; with the traveling-wraps there was no cold. And if it had not been for the thoughts of the absent all would have slept well.

At day-break, about four o'clock, M. de Lauranay came out of the berline, and offered to take my place, so that I might get an hour or two's sleep. Fearing to annoy him if I still refused, I consented, and with my fists in my eyes, and my head in my frock, I had a good sound nap.

At half past six we were all afoot. "Are you not tired, Monsieur Natalis?" asked Mlle. Martha.

"I," said I, "I have slept like a dormouse, while your father kept guard!"

"Natalis exaggerates a little," replied M. de Lauranay, with a smile, "and to-night he will allow me — "

"I will allow you nothing, Monsieur de Lauranay. It would look well for the master to watch through the night while the servant — "

"Servant!" exclaimed Mlle. Martha. "Yes! Servant! Coachman! See here! Am I not a coachman, and a good one, too, I flatter myself! Call me postilion, if you like, so as not to hurt my feelings. I am none the less your servant — "

"No. You are our friend," said Mlle. Martha, holding out her hand; "and the most faithful friend that Heaven could have given us to take us back to France."

Ah! brave lady! What would men not do for people who speak like that, and in a tone of such friendship. As for me, if the chance came for me again to help her — Sufficit! And if I had to give my life for her — Amen! as the cur6 of our village would say.

By seven o'clock we were off. If the day brought no more obstacles than the last, we should before night have traversed Thuringia. It began well. The early hours brought hard work, it is true, for the road mounted between the ridges so sharply that we had to push up the wheels. At noon we had reached the highest part of the defile they call the Gebaiier, if my memory does not deceive me, and which crosses the highest point of the ridge. Thence we had only to go down. Without going full gallop, which would not be prudent, we could go fast.

The weather continued to be stormy. If the rain had not fallen since sunrise, the sky was covered with big clouds resembling enormous bombs. Only a shock was required to make them flash, and then we should have a storm, and storms are always dangerous in mountainous countries. In fact, about six o'clock we could hear the rolling of the thunder some distance off, but approaching very fast.

Mlle. Martha, leaning back in the berline, absorbed in thought, did not seem to be much frightened. My sister shut her eyes and remained motionless.

"Had we not better halt?" asked M. de Lauranay, leaning out of the window.

"I think so," answered I, "and I will do so when I come to a comfortable place to camp. But on this slope that is hardly possible."

"Be careful, Natalis."

"Never fear, Monsieur de Lauranay."

I had hardly finished the words when a mighty flash enveloped the berline and the horses. The lightning had struck an enormous birch-tree on our right. Fortunately the tree was struck on the side away from the road.

The horses became violently excited. I felt I had lost all power over them. They dashed down the defile at full gallop, despite all I could do to stop them. They and I were blinded by the flashes and deafened by the peals of thunder. If the frightened beasts swerved, the berline would be hurled into the ravine by the road-side. Suddenly the reins broke. The horses feeling their liberty dashed ahead still more furiously. An inevitable catastrophe was imminent.

Suddenly there was a shock. The berline had struck against the trunk of a tree that lay across the defile. The traces broke. The horses leaped over the tree. Just at the spot the defile made a sharp turn, and beyond it the unfortunate beasts disappeared in the abyss.

The berline was damaged by the shock, broken in the front wheels, but it was not overturned. M. de Lauranay, Mlle. Martha, and my sister escaped without a wound. I had been thrown out of the saddle, but I was safe and sound.

What an irreparable accident! What was to become of us now, without means of transport, in the middle of this Thurmgian desert: What a night we passed!

Next morning, that of the 23d of August, we had to abandon the berline, which we could not make use of again, even if other horses replaced those we had lost.

I had made up a bundle of provisions and things, that I carried over my shoulder at the end of a stick. We descended the narrow defile which, unless M. de Lauranay was mistaken, opened out on to the plain. I walked in front. My sister and the others followed as well as they could. I do not think we did more than three leagues that day. When we halted for the night the setting sun lighted up the vast plains, stretching away westward from the foot of the mountains of Thuringia.

CHAPTER XVI

The position was serious, and it would become worse if we found no means of replacing the berline we had abandoned in the defiles of the Thuringer Wald!

But the first thing was to find a refuge for the night. Then we could think over matters.

I was in a fix. There was not a cottage to be seen. I did not know what to do until, on going up to the right, I perceived a sort of hut at the edge of the forest on the last spur of the hills.

The hut was open to the winds on three of its sides. Its rotten planks let through the rain and wind, but the shingles on the roof were sound and would keep off the wet if it came on to rain.

The storm of the night before had so cleared the sky that we had no rain during the day. Unfortunately, with the evening thick clouds had returned from the west, and overhead were banking up until they seemed to touch the ground. I considered myself lucky to have found this hut, wretched as it was, now that the berline was gone.

M. de Lauranay had been much affected by the accident, particularly for the sake of his granddaughter. We were still a long way from the French frontier. How would we finish the journey, and in the allotted time, if we had to do it on foot? We had thus many things to think of. But at first we had to attend to the most pressing.

In the interior of the hut, which did not seem to have been recently occupied, the ground was covered with a litter of dry herbs. Perhaps it was a refuge for the shepherds who brought their flocks to feed on the mountains. Below the hill lay the plains of Saxony in the direction of the Fulda, and the province of the Upper Rhine.

Under the rays of the setting sun, which slanted down on to them, the plains rose to the horizon in gentle undulations. Although they were ridged with hills, the road through them was nothing like so difficult as that by which we had come from Gotha.

When night came I helped my sister to get the supper ready. M. and Mlle, de Lauranay were probably overtired, for they could eat nothing. Neither could Irma touch anything. Fatigue had driven away hunger.

"You are wrong," said I. "Eat first and sleep afterward, that is the way with a soldier in the field. We shall have need of our legs now. Mademoiselle Martha, you should take something — "

"I would, good Natalis," said she, "but it is impossible! To-morrow, before we start, I will try — "

"That will be a meal the less!" was my answer.

"Exactly, but never fear. I will not delay you on the road."

For all I could say I did no good, although I preached by example, and eat heartily. I had resolved to give myself the strength of the four, as I expected a quadruple task in the morning.

A few steps from the hut ran a limpid stream, which lost itself in a narrow gorge. A few drops of this water mixed with schnapps from my flask gave me a comforting drink.

Mlle. Martha consented to take two or three mouthfuls. M. de Lauranay and my sister followed her example — and they were right.

Then all three went and lay down in the hut, when they were soon fast asleep.

I had promised to sleep too, intending to do nothing of the sort. I said so because M. de Lauranay would have sat up with me, and it would not do to let him do so.

There I was then, pacing backward and forward like a sentinel. There is nothing new in sentry-go for a soldier. As a matter of prudence the two pistols I had brought from the berline were at my belt. I thought it was best to keep guard properly.

I had firmly resolved not to fall asleep, although my eyelids were heavy. When my legs failed me, I could sit down near the hut with ear and eyes well open.

The night was very dark, although the low mists had gradually floated into the sky. There was not a rift in the thick veil, not a sign of a star. The moon had set soon after the sun. The horizon was, however, clear of fog. If a fire had been lighted in the depths of the forest or on the surface of the plain, I should certainly have seen it. But all was dark in front over the fields, behind over the woods that came down the neighboring ridge and stopped at the angle of the hut. The silence was as deep as the darkness. Not a whisper troubled the calm of the atmosphere, as often happens in such weather when the storm can not even spend itself in mere heat-flashes.

There was a noise, however! There was a whistling that reproduced the calls and sounds of the Royal Picardy Regiment. Natalis Delpierre was at his bad habits, as you may guess. But he was the only whistler at a time when the birds slept under the foliage of the birches and oaks.

And as I whistled I thought of the past. I ran over what had happened at Belzingen since my arrival — the wedding put off, the meeting that did not take place with Lieutenant von Grawert, the recruiting of M. Jean, and our expulsion from German territory. Then in the future I saw the difficulties that were gathering round, Jean Keller with a price on his head flying with a ball at his feet, the ball being a sentence of death, his mother knowing not where to find him!

And if he were found! If some scoundrel did hand him over to pocket this prize of a thousand florins! No! I could not believe it! Bold and resolute M. Jean was not the man to let himself be taken or sold.

While I abandoned myself to these reflections I felt my eyelids shut in spite of me. I got up, not wishing to yield to sleep. I was sorry that nature was so calm during the night, and that the obscurity was so profound. There was not a sound to interest me, not a light over the country or in the sky to attract my attention. And it required a constant effort of will to keep myself from yielding to fatigue.

But the time slipped away. What o'clock might it be? Was it past midnight? Perhaps, for the nights were short at this time of year. And I looked for the sky to get paler in the east over the crest of the mountains. But nothing showed the approach of dawn. I must have been wrong — and I was wrong.

It then occurred to me that during the day M. de Laurnay and I, after consulting the map, had discovered that the first town of importance we should come to would be Tann, in the district of Cassel, in the province of Hesse Nassau. There we might be able to replace the berline. It did not matter how we managed to get to France, providing we got there. To reach Tann we should have to journey about a dozen leagues, and I was deep in my thoughts of this, when I gave a sudden start.

I jumped up and listened. It seemed as though I had heard a distant report. Was it the sound of a musket?

Almost immediately a second report reached me. There was no doubt now; it must be either a musket or a pistol. And I even thought I saw a flash among the trees behind the hut.

In our position in an almost deserted country, there was a good deal to fear. A band of camp followers or pillagers might be passing along the road, and we might be discovered. Even half a dozen men would be too much for us.

A quarter of an hour elapsed. I had not woke up M. de Lauranay. It might be that the report came from some hunter of the wild boar or roebuck. In any case, by the light I saw I reckoned he was half a league away from us.

I stood upright, motionless, looking fixedly toward the spot from whence the sound had come. As I heard nothing I began to be more confident, to ask myself if I had not been the plaything of an illusion of ear and eye. Sometimes you sleep when you do not think you are

101

sleeping. The thing you take for a reality is but the fugitive impression of a dream.

I resolved to fight against this tendency to sleep, and I began to march backward and forward, whistling my loudest calls. I even went into the angle of the forest behind the hut for about a hundred yards under the trees.

Then I seemed to hear a sound of gliding through the underwood. It might be a fox; or it might be a wolf. My pistol was loaded, and ready for him, and such is the force of habit that at this moment, at the risk of betraying my presence, I kept on whistling — as I learned later on.

Suddenly I thought I saw a shadow leap. I fired almost at hazard. But as the report rang out a man rose before me.

In the flash I had recognized him. It was Jean Keller.

CHAPTER XVII

At the noise M. de Lauranay, Mlle. Martha, and my sister suddenly awoke and ran out of the hut. In the man who had come with me out of the forest, they had not recognized M. Jean, nor Mme. Keller who had just come into view immediately behind him. M. Jean rushed toward them. Before he uttered a word Mlle. Martha knew him, and fell into his arms.

"Jean!" she murmured.

"Yes, Martha! And my mother! At last!"

Mlle, de Lauranay sprung into the arms of Mme. Keller.

It would not do to lose our coolness, or do anything imprudent.

"Get back all of you into the hut," said I. "Your head is worth something, Monsieur Jean!"

"What! Do you know?" he said.

"My sister and I know all!"

"And you, Martha, and you, Monsieur de Lauranay?" asked Mme. Keller.

"What is it?" exclaimed Martha.

"You shall learn," said I. "Go back!"

A moment later we were cowering down at the back of the hut. But if we could not be seen we might be heard, and I took up my position so that I could hear all that passed, and yet kept guard over the road.

And this is what M. Jean had to say, interrupting himself only to listen to what was going on outside. He told his story in a panting way, in disjointed phrases which allowed time to take breath, as if he had been thoroughly pumped out by a long run.

"Dearest Martha," said he, "better here — hidden in this hut — than under the orders of Colonel von Grawert and in the same company as Lieutenant Frantz!"

And then in a few words Martha and my sister were told what had happened before our departure from Belzingen, the lieutenant's insulting provocation, the meeting that had been arranged, the refusal to keep the appointment after the call on Jean Keller to join the Leib regiment.

"Yes," said M. Jean, "I was to be under this officer's orders. He could take his vengeance at his ease, instead of standing in front of me, sword in hand. This man, who insulted you, Martha, I would have killed — "

"Jean — my poor Jean!" murmured the girl.

"The regiment was sent to Bonn," continued Jean Keller. "There for a month, I was put to the worst duties that could be found, humiliated in the service, punished unjustly, treated as you would not treat a dog, and by this Frantz. I restrained myself — I bore it all, thinking of you, Martha, and my mother, and all my friends! Ah! what I had to put up with! At last the regiment started for Magdeburg. There my mother was to meet me. But there one evening, five days ago, Lieutenant Frantz met me in a street by myself, overwhelmed me with insults, and struck me with his whip. It was too much. I threw myself on him. I gave him a sound flogging."

"Jean, my poor Jean!" murmured mademoiselle.

"I was lost if I could not escape. Luckily I found my mother at the inn where she was lodging. In a few moments I had changed my uniform for the dress of a peasant, and we had left Magdeburg. Next morning, as I soon knew, I was sentenced to death by a court-martial! A price was put on my head! A thousand florins to whoever would give me up! How could I escape? I did not know! But I had made up my mind to live, Martha — to live and see you all again!"

Here M. Jean broke off.

"Did you hear anything?" he asked.

I slipped out of the hut. The road was silent and deserted. I put my ear to the ground. There was no suspicious sound in the direction of the forest.

"Nothing," said I, as I went back.

"My mother and I were thrown on the fields of Saxony in the hope of joining you, for my mother knew the road the police had ordered you to follow. We traveled at night, buying a little food at isolated houses, passing through villages where I could read the notice offering the reward for my capture — "

"Yes," said I, "the notice my sister and I read at Gotha."

"My plan," continued M. Jean, "was to try and reach Thuringia, where I thought you might still be. There, besides, I should be in more safety. At last we reached the mountains — a rough road, as you know, Natalis, for you have done some of it on foot — "

"Quite so," I replied, "but who told you that?"

"Yesterday evening when we had passed the Gebauer, I noticed a berline half smashed and abandoned on the road. I recognized the carriage as Monsieur de Lauranay's. There had been an accident! Were you safe? Great was our anxiety! My mother and I walked all through the night. Then when day came we had to hide!"

"Hide?" said my sister. "And why? Were you followed?"

"Yes," replied M. Jean, "followed by three scoundrels I met below the Gebauer defile, the poacher Buch of Belzingen and his two sons. I had seen them at Magdeburg, in the rear of the army, with a number of other thieves like them. Doubtless they knew a thousand florins could be gained by following me. This they did, and to-night, hardly two hours ago, we were attacked half a league from here on the edge of the forest — "

"And that accounts for the two reports I thought I heard?"

"They were the two shots they fired. I had my hat shot through by a bullet. However, my mother and I hid in the underwood and escaped the scoundrels. They think we have gone back, for they went on toward the mountains. Then we resumed our road toward the plains, and when we reached the end of the forest, Natalis, I recognized you by your whistling — "

"And I fired at you, Monsieur Jean! I saw a man jump — "

"No matter, Natalis! But the shot may have been heard, and it is better I should be off at once."

"Alone!" exclaimed Mlle. Martha.

"No! we go together!" replied M. Jean. "And if possible we will not part until we have reached the French frontier."

We knew all we need know, that is to say, that M. Jean's life was in danger, if the poacher and his two sons recovered his track. Doubtless we could defend him against these scoundrels. We should not give him up without a struggle! But how would it end if the Buchs were joined by other gentry of their species, such as were then so numerous?

In a few words M. Jean was informed of all that had happened since we left Belzingen, and how the journey had been favored until the accident in the Gebaiier.

Now the want of horses and carriage caused us great embarrassment.

"We must at all cost procure means of transport," said M. Jean.

"I hope we shall be able to find them at Tann," answered M. de Lauranay. "But do not let us stop any longer in this hut. Buch and his sons may not have gone away from the neighborhood. We must take advantage of the night."

"Can you come with us, Martha?" asked M. Jean.

"I am ready," said Mlle, de Lauranay.

"And you, mother, can you bear such fatigues?"

"Forward, my son!" answered Mme. Keller.

We had some provisions left; enough to take us to Tann. That would save us halting in the villages where Buch might pass or had passed.

Before we started we talked over what was best to be done, for, as we say at picquet, it is best to make sure of the baby. Although it was not without danger, we decided to keep together. That would be relatively easy for M. and Mlle, de Lauranay, my sister and I, inasmuch as our passports protected us up to the French frontier, but it would not be easy for Mme. Keller aud her son. They must be careful not to enter the villages we were obliged to pass through; they must leave us before we get to them. In this way it was not impossible for us to travel together.

"Let us be off," said I. "If I can buy a carriage and horses at Tann, there will be a good many fatigues spared your mother and Mademoiselle Martha, and my sister and Monsieur de Lauranay. As to us, Monsieur Jean, we have only a few days' march for us to see how beautiful the stars shine on the fair land of France."

And I was off, twenty yards on the road. It was two o'clock in the morning. Darkness enveloped the whole country. But on the crests of the mountains, the first pale streaks of dawn were just growing visible.

If I could see nothing I could hear. I listened attentively. The air was so calm that the sound of a footstep on the road or in the thicket could not have escaped me.

Nothing! We could conclude that Buch and his son had lost the trail of Jean Keller.

We were all out of the hut. I was carrying what remained of our provisions, and believe me the weight was not a great one. One of our pistols I had given to M.

Jean; the other I kept. When the time came we knew how to use them.

At this moment Jean took Mlle, de Lauranay's hand, and in a voice of great emotion said to her: "Martha! when I wished to make you my wife, my life was my own! Now I am a fugitive condemned to death! I have no right to associate your life with mine."

"Jean, we are one in the sight of God! May He protect us!"

CHAPTER XVIII

i will pass rapidly over the first two days of our journey with Mme. Keller and her son. We had the good luck in leaving Thuringia to meet with no adventure.

We were much excited, and we went along at a good pace. Fatigue seemed to have no power over us. Mme. Keller, Mlle. Martha, and my sister wished to set us an example. We had to quiet them down a little. We rested one hour in every four during the day.

The country was not very fertile and was cut up by sinuous ravines, bristling with willows and aspens — a wild place is this part of Hesse Nassau, which has since been formed into the district of Cassel. There are few villages, only a few flat-roofed farms. We crossed the little river of Schmalkalden in favorable weather, with a clear sky and a pleasant fresh breeze that blew us onward. Nevertheless, our companions were tired enough when on the 24th of August, after a dozen leagues on foot from the mountains of Thuringia, we arrived at Tann about ten o'clock at night.

Then, as had been agreed, M. Jean and his mother separated from us. It was not prudent to enter a town where he might be recognized, and we knew what that meant!

He had appointed to meet us in the morning about eight o'clock on the road to Fulda. If we were not punctual it would be because the acquisition of a carriage and horses had delayed us. But under no pretext were Mme. Keller and her son to enter Tann. And that was wise, for the police were very strict in examining our passports. I saw the time coming when they would detain the people they were expelling. We had to tell them how we were traveling, how we lost our carriage, etc.

That did us some good, however. One of the police, in the hope of a good commission, offered to introduce us to a jobmaster. His proposition was accepted. After taking Mlle. Martha and my sister to the hotel, M. de Lauranay, who spoke German well, went with me to the man.

A traveling carriage he had not. We had to be content with a sort of two-wheeled wagon covered with a tilt, drawn by one horse. I need not add that M. de Lauranay had to pay twice the value of the horse, and three times that of the wagon.

At eight o'clock next morning we found Mme. Keller and her son on the road. They had slept at a dirty inn. M. Jean had passed the night in a chair, while his mother had slept on a pallet. M. and Mlle, de Lauranay, Mme. Keller and Irma got into the wagon, where I had packed some provisions bought at Tann. By sitting close another place was left, which I offered to M. Jean. He refused it, and finally it was agreed we should take it in turns, and most of the time it happened that we both walked to make things easy for the horse.

On the 26th we reached Fulda, after seeing from afar the dome of its cathedral, and on a height a convent of Franciscans. On the 27th we went through Schlinchtern, Sodon, Salmunster, at the junction of the Salza and the Kinzig. On the 28th we reached Gelnhausen, and if we had been traveling for pleasure we should have visited the castle inhabited by Frederick Barbarossa, as they told me afterward. But fugitives, or little better than fugitives, had something else to do.

The wagon did not go as fast as I liked, owing to the bad state of the road, which principally in the neighborhood of Salmunster runs through interminable forests with huge fish-ponds, such as we call cuts in Picardy. We could only go at a foot-pace; and the delay was getting serious. We had been thirteen days on the road; in seven more days our passports would be worthless.

Mme. Keller was almost tired out. What would happen if her strength gave out, and we had to leave her in some town or village? Her son could not remain with her. Until the French frontier was between M. Jean and the Prussian police he was in danger of his life.

110

What difficulties we had in the forest of Lomberg, which extends from the left to the right of Kinzig to the mountains of Hesse Darmstadt! I thought we should never get to the other side of the river; and we had to lose a lot of time before we found a ford.

On the 29th the wagon stopped a little short of Hanau. We ought to have passed the night in this town, where there was a considerable movement going on of troops and transport. As M. Jean and his mother would have had to make a circuit of two leagues to avoid it, M. de Lauranay and Mlle. Martha remained with them in the wagon. My sister and I went alone into the town to replenish our stores; and we joined them in the morning of the 30th on the road that runs through Wiesbaden. At noon we avoided the little town of Offenbach, and in the evening we reached Frankfort-on-the-Main.

Of this large city I shall say nothing, except that it is on the right bank of the river, and that it swarms with Jews. Having crossed the Main in the ferry-boat from Offenbach we were on the road to Mayence. But as we could not avoid entering Frankfort to get our passports examined, we went in, and complied with the order, and then came

back again, so that that night we were not separated. And what we appreciated even more was that we found a modest but very comfortable lodging in the suburb of Sahlsenhausen, on the left bank of the Main.

After supper together they all went to bed, while my sister and I went out to make a few purchases.

Among other things Irma heard people talking at the baker's about Jean Keller. They said he had been captured near Salmunster, and the details of his capture were not given. We might have been amused at this had we been in the humor. But we heard something else that seemed to me to be very serious indeed. And that was that the Leib regiment was expected to march through Frankfort to Mayence, and so on to Thionville. If that was true, Colonel von Grawert and his son would be on the same road as we were. Would it not be better, then, to change our route at the risk of getting into trouble for avoiding the towns indicated by the Prussian police?

In the morning of the 31st I told M. Jean this unwelcome news. He advised me to say nothing about it to his mother or Mlle. Martha, who already had enough to worry them. Beyond Mayence we could talk over what had better be done, and, if need be, separate until we got to the frontier. By pressing forward we might gain on the Leib regiment.

We started at six o'clock. Unfortunately, the road was difficult and fatiguing. We had to go through the forests of Neilruh and La Ville, which border on Frankfort. There was a delay of some hours in turning the villages of Hochst and Hochheim, which were full of a transport-train. I saw the time coming when our old wagon and its bony horse would be taken for the transport of many a hundred-weight of bread. Although we were only fifteen leagues from Frankfort it was not till the evening of the 31st that we reached Mayence. We were then on the frontier of Hesse Darmstadt.

It will be guessed that Mme. Keller and her son had good reason for avoiding Mayence. The town is on the left bank of the Rhine, at the junction of the Main, and opposite Cassel, which is practically one of its suburbs, and is connected with it by a bridge of boats six hundred feet long.

To strike the roads to France we had necessarily to cross the Rhine, either above or below the town, or go over the bridge. We therefore went off in search of a boat to take over M. Jean and his mother. Our search was useless. All boats were forbidden to cross by the military authorities.

It was then eight o'clock in the evening. We did not know what to do.

"My mother and I must get over the Rhine somehow," said Jean Keller.

"And where and how?" asked I.

"By the bridge of Mayence, if it is impossible to cross anywhere else."

And then the following plan was adopted: M. Jean took my frock, which covered him from head to foot. Holding the horse by the bridle he walked toward the gate of Cassel.

Mme. Keller was hidden in the back of the wagon under our traveling-wraps. M. and Mlle, de Lauranay and my sister and I occupied the two seats. In this way we approached the old ramparts with their mossy walls, between the advanced parties, and the wagon stopped at the guard at the head of the bridge.

There was a great crowd of people coming home from the free-market held that day at Mayence. M. Jean put a bold face on the matter.

"Your passports?" they asked.

I held out the passports, which were handed on to the commander of the guard.

"Who are these people?" he asked.

"French subjects I am taking to the frontier."

'' And who are you?"

"Nicholas Friedel, jobmaster at Hochst."

Our passports were examined with extreme attention. Although they were all in order you can imagine the state of mind we were in.

"These passports have only four days to run," said the commander of the guard. "In four days you must be off German territory."

"They shall be," said Jean Keller, "but we have no time to lose."

"Pass!"

Half an hour afterward the Rhine was crossed, and we were at the Anhalt Hotel, where M. Jean could play his part of jobmaster to his heart's content.

How strange things are! What a different reception would have awaited us a few months later, when, in October, Mayence surrendered to the French! What joy there would have been at our finding our countrymen there! How they would have welcomed us! And if we had stopped six months, eight months, in this capital, we would have gone out with our brave regiments and the honors of war to return to France.

But you do not always arrive when you like, and the chief thing is to be able to get away when you like.

When Mme. Keller, Mlle. Martha and Irma had gone to their rooms at the Anhalt Hotel, M. Jean went to look after his horse; and M. de Lauranay and I went out in search of news.

The best thing to be done was to go to a public-house and ask for the latest papers; and it was worth the trouble to find out what had happened in France since our departure. What had happened was the terrible 10th of August, the invasion of the Tuileries, the massacre of the Swiss, the shutting up of the royal family in the Temple, and the provisional deposition of royalty.

That was enough, at all events, to hurl the masses of the Coalition on the French frontier.

And France was already prepared to resist the invasion.

She had three armies. Luckner was in the north, Lafayette was in the center, Montesquieu was in the south Dumouriez was serving under Luckner as lieutenant-general.

But — the news was only three days old — Lafayette, with some of his companions, had visited the Austrian headquarters, and in spite of his protest, had been detained as a prisoner of war.

From that we could judge of the disposition of our enemies toward everything that was French, and the fate that awaited us if we were taken without passports.

114

Doubtless on what the newspapers said there was much to give and take. However, this was how things stood at that moment.

Dumouriez, the real commander-in-chief of the armies of the north and center, was a master man, as you know. Desirous of dealing him the first blow, the Kings of Prussia and Austria came to Mayence. The Duke of Brunswick was in command of the armies of the Coalition. After penetrating France through the Ardennes, they were to march on Paris by way of Chalons. A column of sixty thousand Prussians was advancing through Luxemburg on Longwy. Thirty - six thousand Austrians, in two corps, under the orders of Clairfayt and Prince Hohenlohe, flanked the Prussian army. Such were the terrible masses that threatened France.

I tell you now what I learned afterward, so that you may understand the position of things. Dumouriez was at Sedan with twenty-three thousand men. Kellermann, replacing Luckner, was at Metz with twenty thousand. Fifteen thousand were at Landau, under Custine; thirty thousand were in Alsace under Biron, and ready to join either Dumouriez or Kellermann as might be required.

The last news in the gazettes told us that the Prussians had taken Longwy; that they were blockading Thionville, and the bulk of their army was marching on Verdun.

We returned to the hotel, and when Mme. Keller knew what had happened, she refused to wait a day at Mayence, although she was very feeble, and rest was almost imperative for her. But she trembled lest her sou should be discovered. So we started next morning, that of the 1st of September. Thirty leagues still separated us from the frontier.

Our horse, notwithstanding all I could do, did not go quickly. And how time was pressing! It was evening when we sighted the ruins of the old castle on the Schloss- berg. At the foot lay Kreuznach, an important town of the district of Coblenz, situated on the Nahe, and which, after belonging to France in 1801, was returned to Prussia in 1815.

The next morning we reached the village of Kirn, and twenty-four hours afterward that of Birkenfeld. Fortunately provisions did not fail us, and we were able to get round these towns which were not mentioned on our itinerary. But the wagon was our only shelter, and the nights passed under such circumstances could not but be uncomfortable.

It was the same when we halted on the 3d of September. On the morrow at midnight would expire the time allowed us for evacuating German territory. And we were still two days' march from the frontier! What would become of us if we were stopped on the road without passports that the Prussian would recognize?

Perhaps we had better turn off toward the south, toward Sarrelouis, the nearest French town. But that was to risk falling into the hands of the Prussians coming up to re-enforce the blockade of Thionville. And it was better to lengthen our route to avoid that dangerous meeting.

In short, we were only a few leagues from the frontier, and all were safe and sound. That M. and Mlle, de Lauranay and my sister and I had reached here was not very extraordinary, but that Mme. Keller and her son had got so far was much to be thankful for. When Jean Keller joined our party in the mountains of Thuringia, I hardly thought we should shake hands on the frontier of France.

But we had to avoid Saarbriilck, not only for the sake of M. Jean and his mother, but for our own. It would be more likely to offer us the hospitality of a prison than of a hotel.

We spent the night at an inn, whose customary guests were not of first quality. More than once the innkeeper looked at us in a strange way. It seemed to me that when we left he exchanged a few words with some people seated in a small room out of our sight.

On the 4th of September we took the road which passes between Thionville and Metz, ready, if need be, to bear off to Metz, which the French then occupied.

An uncomfortable road it was through the patches of woodland scattered hereabouts. The poor horse was nearly knocked up, and about two o'clock in the afternoon, at the foot of a long hill running up behind thick brushwood, and bordered here and there by fields of hops, we had all to get down, all except Mme. Keller, who was too fatigued to leave the wagon.

We were advancing slowly. I held the horse by the bridle. My sister was near me. M. de Lauranay, his granddaughter and M. Jean were a little behind. Except ourselves, there was no one on the road. Far off we could hear heavy firing. Doubtless the fighting was going on under the walls of Thionville.

Suddenly on our right there was the report of a gun. Our horse, mortally wounded, fell between the shafts, which broke. At the same time there were shouts.

"We have got them at last!"

"Yes. That is Jean Keller!"

"We have got the thousand florins!"

"Not yet!" said M. Jean.

There was a second report. This time it was M. Jean who had fired, and a man rolled on the ground near our horse.

It all took place so quickly that I had not time to pull myself together.

"They are the Buchs!" said M. Jean.

"Well! Book them, then!" said I.

The rascals had been at the inn where we had passed the night. After a few words with the innkeeper they had followed on our track.

But of three only two were left, the father and second son. The other, with a bullet through his heart, was just dying.

Two against two was equal. But the fight did not last long. I aimed at young Buch, but I only wounded him. Then his father and he, seeing their stroke had failed, jumped into the thicket on the left and scuttled off.

I was going in chase. M. Jean stopped me. May be he was wrong.

"No," said he, "the best thing is to get over the frontier! Come on! Come on!"

As we had no horse left we had to abandon our wagon. Mme. Keller had to get down and rest on her son's arm.

In a few hours our passports would not protect us!

Thus we went on till the night. We camped under the trees. We eat the last of our provisions. Next day, the 5th of September, in the evening we crossed the frontier.

Yes! It was Franch soil we then trod! But the French soil was occupied by foreign soldiers!

CHAPTER XIX

We were near the end of this long journey which the declaration of war had obliged us to make across the enemy's country; this painful road to France we had traversed at the cost of such extreme fatigue and danger. Except on two or three occasions — among others when the Buchs attacked us — our lives had never been in peril, nor had our liberty.

What I say of ourselves applies equally to M. Jean since we had met him in the Thuringian mountains. Now all he had to do was to find some town in the Low Countries where he could watch in safety the issue of events.

But the frontier was invaded. Austrians and Prussians in possession of this region, extending to the forest of Argonne, made it as dangerous for us as if we were in the districts of Potsdam or Brandenburg. After the fatigues of the past the future had reserved dangers as great for us.

What would you have? You think you have reached your journey's end and you are only on the road.

Before we could pass the advance-posts of the enemy and his cantonments we had twenty leagues to go. But in marches and counter-marches how long might not that become?

Perhaps it would have been better to have entered France to the south or north of Lorraine. In our state, however, deprived of all means of transport, with no hope of procuring any, we had to think twice before going out of the direct road.

M. de Lauranay, M. Jean and I had debated the question, and after discussing the pros and cons, we saw reason to abandon my proposition.

It was eight o'clock in the evening when we reached the frontier. Before us was a thick wood, through which it was not wise to venture during the night. We halted till the morning. It might not rain on these elevated places; but in the beginning of September the cold would make itself felt. As to lighting a fire, that would be too imprudent for fugitives who wished to get through unper- ceived. We hid ourselves as well as we could under the lower branches of a beech-tree. The provisions I had brought from the wagon — the bread, and cold meat, and cheese — were on our knees. A brook gave us clear water which we mixed with a few drops of schnapps. Then leaving M. de Lauranay, Mme. Keller, Mlle. Martha, and my sister to take a few hours' rest, M. Jean and I went about ten yards away.

M. Jean was much absorbed, and did not at first speak, and I respected his silence. At last he said: "Listen, Natalis, and never forget what I am going to tell you. We do not know what may happen — to me especially. I may be forced to escape. Well, my mother need not leave you. The poor woman is almost dead; and if I am compelled to separate from you I do not wish her to follow me. You see how she is, in spite of her energy and courage. I intrust her to you then, Natalis, as I do Martha; that is to say, all I hold dearest in this world!"

"You can depend upon me, Monsieur Jean. I hope nothing will separate us! However, if it does happen, I will do all you can expect from a man who is entirely faithful to you."

M. Jean clasped my hand.

"Natalis! if they catch me I have no doubt as to my fate! It will soon be over! Remember, then, that my mother must never return to Prussia. She was French before her marriage. Her husband and her son will be no more, and she should end her life in the country in which she was born."

"She was French, you say, Monsieur Jean? Say rather she is French and has never ceased to be so in our eyes."

"Be it so, Natalis! Take her with you to your own Picardy that I have never seen and wish so much to see. Let us hope that my mother, in default of happiness, may find there the rest which is her due! Poor woman! How great have been her sufferings!"

And had not M. Jean much to suffer?

"Ah! this country!" continued he. "If we had been able to come here together, Martha, my wife, and my mother, and I, how soon we should have forgotten our troubles. But am I not mad to dream of such things? I, a fugitive, a convict whom death may strike at any moment!"

"Wait, Monsieur Jean, do not speak like that! They have not got you yet, and I shall be much surprised if you are the man to be taken!"

"No, Natalis! I shall fight to the last, depend upon that!"

"And I'll help you, Monsieur Jean!"

"I know it, my friend. Let me embrace you. It is the first time I am allowed to clasp in my arms a Frenchman on the soil of France!"

"And it will not be the last!" said I.

Yes! The depth of confidence that was in me had never been shaken, notwithstanding our trials. It was not without reason that I was considered at Grattepanche to be one of the most obstinate addlepates in all Picardy.

But night was passing. Each in turn, M. Jean and I, had a rest. It was so dark, so dark under the trees, that nothing could be seen of us. When I was on guard I listened with my ear against the wind; the least noise made me suspicious. Amid these woods we had to fear, not so much the soldiers of the regular army as the camp followers, as we clearly saw in the affair with the Buchs.

Unfortunately, two of these Buchs had escaped us. Their first care would be to recapture us; and to succeed they would probably bring with ihem a few rascals like them to share in the thousand florins.

Yes! I thought of all this, and it kept me awake. I thought also that if the Leib regiment had left Frankfort twenty-four hours after us it might have crossed the frontier. Might it not be in the neighborhood, in the forest of Argonue?

These apprehensions were exaggerated without doubt. And is it not always thus when the brain is overexcited? That was my case. I thought I heard marching among the trees. I seemed to see shadows gliding among the thickets. I need not say that if M. Jean was armed with one of the pistols, I had the other in my belt, and we were resolved to let no one come near us.

But the night passed without an alarm. Many times we heard distant trumpet-calls, and even the roll of drums, which toward morning beat the reveille. The sounds came from the south, and indicated a cantonment of troops.

Probably they were Austrian columns waiting to march on Thionville, or even on Montmedy, more to the north. As I have since heard, the intention of the allies was not to capture these places, but to mask them, to paralyze their garrisons, so as to cross unhindered the territory of the Ardennes.

We might run up against a column of these troops, and we should then soon be done for. Austrians or Prussians would be all the same to us. One would be as bad as the other.

We decided to bear off to the north in the direction of Stenay, or even of Sedan, so as to get right into the forest, but away from the road likely to be followed by the Imperialists.

At day-break we started.

The weather was beautiful. We heard the whistling of the bullfinches, and on the edge of the clearings the grasshoppers chirping in sign of warmth; then afar the skylarks trilling their sweet song as they mounted straight in the air.

We went along as fast as the weakness of Mme. Keller permitted. Under the thick leafage of the trees the sun had no power over us. What worried me was that our provisions were running out. And how could we replace them?

As agreed, we headed a little to the northward, far from such villages and hamlets as the enemy would certainly have occupied.

The day was distinguished by no adventure. The distance we covered in a direct line was not great. In the afternoon Mme. Keller gave up entirely. She whom I had known at Belzingen straight as an ash was now bent, her legs gave way as she walked, and I saw the time coming when she could go no further.

During the night the distant firing was heard continuously. It was artillery, and in the direction of Verdun.

The country we were crossing consisted of woods of no great size, and plains watered by numerous streams. They were but brooks in the dry season, and we could easily cross them. As much as possible we walked under the shelter of the trees, so as to throw pursuers off our trail.

Four days before, on the 2d of September, as we afterward learned, Verdun, so gallantly defended by the heroic Beaurepaire, who committed suicide rather than surrender, had opened its gates to fifty thousand Prussians. This occupation allowed the Coalition to muster their forces on the plains of the Meuse. Brunswick contented himself by taking Stenay, while Dumouriez — artful fellow! — who was secretly preparing his plan of resistance, remained at Sedan.

To return to what concerns us, and which we did not know, it was on the 30th of August — eight days before — Dillon had slipped with eight thousand men between the Argonne and the Meuse. After driving Clairfayt and his Austrians, who then occupied both banks of the river, to the other side, he had advanced so as to seize the southerly entrance to the forest.

If we had known that, instead of going to the north we should have made straight for this entrance. There, among French soldiers, our safety would have been assured. But there was nothing to tell us of this maneuver, and it seemed to be our fate to run into danger.

Next day, 7th of September, we exhuasted our provisions. Cost what they might, we must get some more. The evening came. An isolated house was seen at the side of a pond on the edge of a wood near an old stone wall. There was no room to hesitate. I knocked at the door. It was opened to us. We were among honest country people. At first these people told us that although the Prussians remained quiet in their cantonments the Austrians were expected on that side. As to the French, the rumor ran that Dumouriez had left Sedan to join Dillon, and was descending between the Argonne and the Meuse, so as to drive Brunswick over the frontier.

This was a mistake, as will be seen immediately; but the mistake fortunately did us no harm.

The hospitality offered us by the peasants was as complete as possible in the deplorable condition that they then were in. A good fire — what we call a battle fire — was lighted on the hearth, and we made a good meal of eggs and fried sausages, a large hunch of rye bread, a few of those aniseed-cakes that they call "kisch "in Lorraine, some green apples, and a little white wine of the Moselle.

We also bought provisions to last us for a few days, not forgetting tobacco, of which I was getting short. M. de Lauranay had some trouble in getting our hosts to accept what was their due. This gave Jean Keller a foretaste of the good-heartedness of the French. After a night's rest we were off next day with the dawn.

It seemed indeed as though nature had accumulated diffi-

culties on our road, gaps in the ground, impenetrable thickets, quagmires, in which we almost sunk to our middles. There was no footpath that we could safely follow. There were thick scrubs, such as I had seen in the New World before the ax of the pioneer had done its work. Sometimes in little hollows in the trees stood little statues of the Virgin and saints. At long intervals we met a few shepherds, goatherds, woodmen with their felt kneecaps, or swineherds leading their sows to the acorn-grounds. As soon as they caught sight of us they turned off into the thickets, and if we obtained information once or twice, that was all.

We also heard file firing, indicating a fight of outposts.

We got near to the Stenay, although the obstacles were so great and the fatigues such that we hardly did two leagues a day. It was the same during the 9th, 10th, and 11th of September; but though the ground was difficult it afforded us complete security. We met with nothing at which we could take alarm. We had no fear of hearing the terrible "Wer da?" which is the Prussian qui-vive.

In taking this direction we were in the' hopes of joining the army under Dumouriez. But, as we had no means of knowing, he had already gone southward, so as to occupy the defile of Grand Pre, in the forest of Argonne.

Every now and then, I repeat, we could hear the sounds of firing. When they approached us we halted. Evidently no battalion was then engaged on the borders of the Meuse. They were simple attacks on villages, as we supposed from the columns of smoke that mounted above the trees, and the distant gleams of fire in the obscurity of the woods.

In the evening of the 11th we came to a resolution to stop our march on Stenay, and plunge into the Argonne.

Next day we did so. We dragged along, helping each other as we went. The sight of the poor women, so courageous, but so miserable-looking, with faces livid and wan, and clothes in rags, struggling through the holly and thorns, almost drove us to despair.

About noon we reached an opening in the wood, from which we could look over a considerable extent of country.

There, there had recently been a fight. Dead men lay on the ground. I recognized them by their blue uniforms with red lapels, white gaiters, and white crossbelts, so different from the sky-blue Prussians, or the white Austrians with the pointed caps.

They were French volunteers, who had been surprised by some column of Clairfayt's or Brunswick's. They had not given up without a struggle. A certain number of Germans were lying near them, and some of them were Prussians with their copper shakos and chains.

I went up to the heap of corpses and looked at it with horror, for never have I been able to accustom myself to the sight of a battle-field.

Suddenly I uttered a cry. M. de Lauranay, Mme. Keller and her son, Mlle. Martha and my sister, stopped on the edge of the trees, about fifty yards behind me, looking at me, and not daring to advance into the middle of the clearing.

M. Jean came running up to me.

"What is the matter, Natalis?"

Ah! how I regretted that I had not restrained myself! I tried to drag M. Jean away. It was too late. In an instant he had guessed why I had uttered the cry.

A corpse lay at my feet! M. Jean had not to look at it long to recognize it. And then with arms crossed he shook his head.

"Do not let my mother or Martha know."

But Mme. Keller had come out after us, and she saw what we would have hidden, the body of a Prussian soldier, a sergeant of the Leib regiment, stretched on the ground among some thirty of his comrades.

Within the last twenty-four hours, perhaps, the regiment had passed this way, and now it was scouring the country around us. Never had the danger been so great for Jean Keller. If he was captured, his identity would be immediately established, and his execution would take place forthwith.

We must get away from this dangerous place as soon as possible. We must dive into the deepest parts of the Argonne, where a column on the march could not penetrate. There we ought to hide for some days. That was our only chance of safety.

We traveled all that day, and all night.

Traveled? No! Dragged along! The next day, September 13th, we reached the end of this celebrated forest of Argonne, of which Dumouriez had said, "It is the Thermopylae of France, but I shall be more fortunate than Leonidas!"

And so he was. And it was thus that thousands of know-nothings like me learned who was Leonidas, and what was Thermopylae.

CHAPTER XX

The forest of Argonne occupies a space of from thirteen to fourteen leagues, between Sedan on the north, and the little village of Passavant on the south, and it is about three leagues wide on the average. It is like an advanced fortification, covering our frontier on the east with a line that is almost impenetrable. Its woods and streams are mixed up in such extraordinary confusion among heights and valleys, and torrents and pools, that it is almost impossible for troops to cross them.

The forest lies between two rivers. The Aisne borders it on the left, from the furthest thickets in the south to the village of Semuy in the north. The Aire borders it from Fleury up to its chief defile. Then the river makes a sharp bend and returns toward the Aisne into which it flows not far from Senuc.

On the Aire side the chief towns are Clermont, Varennes, where Louis XVI. was arrested when he fled, Buzancy, and Le Chene-Populeux. On the Aisne side are Saint Menehould, Ville-sur-Tourbe, Monthois, and Vouziers.

In shape I can not compare the forest to anything better than a huge insect, with folded wings, motionless or asleep between two streams. Its abdomen will be all the lower part, which is the most important, its" thorax and its head are the upper parts about the Grand Pre defile through which runs the Aire, as I have already said.

If the Argonne is everywhere cut up by water-courses and bristles with thickets, it can, nevertheless, be crossed by different roads, narrow ones, no doubt, but practicable for regiments on the march. It is necessary that I say this here in order that you may understand better what follows.

Five defiles run quite through the Argonne. In the abdomen of my insect, the most southerly one, that of Islettes, goes almost straight from Clermont to Saint Menehould; the next, that of Chalade, is merely a footpath, which joins the bank of the Aisne near Vienne-le-Chateau.

In the upper part of the forest there are no less than three passages. The widest and most important is that which separates the thorax from the abdomen, the defile of Grand Pre. The Aire runs right through it from Saint Juvin, then on between Termes and Senuc, and there joining the Aisne a league and a half from Monthois. Beyond the defile of Grand Pre, hardly two leagues further, is the defile of Croix-aux-Bois — remember this name — crossing the forest of Argonne from Boult-aux-Bois to Longwe. It is but a woodman's road. Two leagues further up is the defile of Chene-Populeux, through which runs the road from Bethel to Sedan, after making two or three bends, and touching the Aisne opposite Vouziers.

It was only by this forest that the Imperialists could advance on Chalons-sur-Marne. From there they would find the road open to Paris.

What had to be done then was to hinder Brunswick or Clairfayt from getting through the Argonne by closing the five defiles that could give access to their columns.

Dumouriez, an able soldier, had seen this at a glance. It seemed to him that it ought to be very easy to do so.

This plan offered the further advantage that it would not be necessary for him to retreat on the Marne, which is our last line of defense before Paris. At the same time, the allies would be compelled to remain in this Champagne-Pouilleux, where everything would fail them, instead of spreading over the rich plains beyond the Argonne during the winter — if they intended to remain during the winter.

He worked out his plan in all its details. And he began its execution on the 30th of August, when Dillon, at the head of eight thousand men, made the bold movement in which, as I have said, the Austrians were driven to the right bank of the Meuse. Then this column took possession of the most southerly defile, that of Islettes, after taking care to guard the defile of Chalade.

There was a certain boldness about these maneuvers. Instead of resting on the Aisne and taking shelter in the thick of the forest, Dillon lay along the Meuse with his flank exposed to the enemy. But Dumouriez had ordered it so in order to hide his scheme from the Coalition.

On the 4th of September, when Dillon reached the defile of Islettes, Dumouriez started after him with fifteen thousand men, and took possession of the defile of Grand Pre, thus closing the chief entrance to the Argonne. Four days afterward General Dubourg appeared at Chene-Populeux so as to defend the north of the forest against any Imperialist invasion.

Immediately the French generals arrived at their stations, they set to work to throw up intrenchments and palisade the footpaths, and establish batteries to close the defiles. The intrenchment at Grand Pre became a regular camp, with the troops stationed round the amphitheater of hills.

At this time, of five of the gates of the Argonne, four were closed like the posterns of a citadel with the portcullis down and draw-bridge up.

But there was a fifth passage left open. This had appeared so little practicable that Dumouriez had been in no hurry to occupy it. And it was toward this very passage that our ill-luck led us.

This defile of Croix-aux-Bois, between Chene-Populeux and Grand Pre, at an equal distance from each — about ten leagues — was to allow the enemy's columns to get through the Argonne.

And now let us return to what concerns ourselves. It was on the evening of the 13th of September that we arrived on the lateral slope of the Argonne, after avoiding the villages of Briquenay and Boult-aux-Bois, which were probably occupied by Austrians.

As I knew the defiles of the Argonne from having been through them many times while in garrison on the east frontier, I had chosen this one of Croix-aux-Bois because I thought it was the safest. But by excess of prudence it was not the defile itself I thought of following, but a narrow footpath near it, which runs from Briquenay to Longwe. By this road, we could cross through the thickest part of the forest beneath oaks, beeches, hornbeams, pines, service trees, willows, and chestnuts which flourish here, where they are less exposed to the snows of winter. By this road we were not likely to meet with many marauders, and we could strike the left bank of the Aisne near Vouziers, where we should have nothing to fear.

The night of the 13th we spent as usual under the shade of the trees.

Any moment there might appear the busby of a dragoon, or the shako of a Prussian grenadier. I therefore did my best to get well into the forest, and I began to breathe more at my ease when next day we struck the footpath to Longwe and left the village of Croix-aux-Bois on our right.

It was a hard day's work. The ground was hilly, with many quagmires and dead trees, and progress was not easy.

The road was almost deserted, probably on account of its being so difficult. M. de Lauranay kept up at a good pace in spite of the great fatigues for a man of his. age. Mlle, de Lauranay aud my sister, at the thought of our being near the end, had made up their minds not to give way for an instant. But Mme. Keller was almost helpless. We had to support her at every step to prevent her falling. But she made no complaint. If the body was exhausted, the spirit remained unsubdued. I doubted if we should reach the end of our journey.

In the evening we halted as usual. The knapsack furnished us with the wherewithal to satisfy our appetites, though hunger had to yield to the want of rest and sleep. When I was alone with M. Jean I spoke to him of the state of his mother, which had become very disquieting.

"She is doing more than she is able," said I, "and if we can not give her a day's rest — "

"So I see, Natalis. Every step she takes is as if she were walking on my heart. What is to be done?"

"We must get to the nearest village, Monsieur Jean. You and I will take her there. Neither Austrians nor Prussians will venture through this part of the Argonne, and in some house we can wait until the country is quieter."

"Yes, Natalis, that is the best thing to do. But could we not reach Longwe?"

"That village is too far off, Monsieur Jean. Your mother would never reach it!"

"Where shall we go, then?"

"Let us strike off to the right through the wood and get to Croix-aux-Bois."

"How far is that?"

"About a league."

"Let us go to Croix-aux-Bois to-morrow, and start at daylight"

Frankly, I did not think there was anything better to do, for I was under the impression that the enemy would never venture in the north of the Argonne.

All through the night, however, we heard the cracking of musketry and from time to time the heavy boom of cannon. But as these reports were distant and came from our rear, I supposed, with some appearance of reason, that Clairfayt or Brunswick was trying to force the defile of Grand Pre, the only one that could offer a sufficient road for the passage of their columns. Neither M. Jean nor I had an hour's rest. We had to be constantly on the qui- vive, although we were in the thick of the wood some distance off the Briquenay footpath.

At day-break we were off. I had cut a few branches with which we made a sort of litter. An armful of dry herbs would allow Mme. Keller to lie upon it, and with great care we might perhaps save her some of the hardships of the road.

But Mme. Keller saw what an increase of fatigue that meant for us.

"No," said she, "no, my son! I am still strong enough to walk. I will go on foot."

"You are not able to!" answered M.. Jean.

"You can not, Madame Keller," said I. "Our idea is to get to the nearest village, and we must get there soon. There we will wait until you are well again. We are in France after all, and no door will be shut against us!"

Mme. Keller would not give in. She rose and tried to take a few steps, but she would have fallen had not her son and my sister caught her and supported her.

"Madame Keller," then said I, "what we desire is safety for all. During the night we heard firing on the outskirts of the Argonne. The enemy is not far off. I am in hopes that he will not come thjs way. At Croix- aux-Bois we need have no fear of surprise, but we must get there to-day."

Mlle. Martha and my sister added their entreaties to ours, M. de Lauranay joined in, and Mme. Keller yielded.

A minute afterward she was lying on the litter that M. Jean lifted at one end while I lifted the other. We began our march, and the Briquenay footpath was crossed obliquely in a northerly direction.

I need not dwell on the difficulties of traveling through a thick wood in this way, or of the frequent halts we had to make. We were through at last, and about noon on the 15th of September we arrived at Croix-aux-Bois, the league and a half having taken us five hours.

To my great astonishment and dismay, the village was abandoned. All the inhabitants had fled either to Vouziers or Chene-Populeux. What then was to be done?

We wandered along the street. Doors and windows were closed. Would the help on which I had reckoned fail us?

"There is some smoke!" said my sister to me, pointing to the end of the village.

I ran toward the little house from which the smoke rose. I knocked at the door.

A man appeared. He had a good face — one of those Lorraine peasant faces that inspire sympathy. He looked like a good fellow.

"What do you want?" he asked.

"Welcome for my companions and myself."

"Who are you?"

"French people driven from Germany, and who do not know where to find a refuge."

"Enter!"

The peasant's name was Hans Stenger. He lived in the house with his mother-in-law and his wife. He had not left Croix-aux-Bois because his mother-in-law could not move from the chair where for many years paralysis had imprisoned her.

And then Hans Stenger told us why the village was abandoned. All the defiles of the Argonne had been occupied by French troops. Only that of Croix-aux-Bois was left open. The Imperialists would thus soon seize on the village, and that meant disaster for us. We had come just where we should not have come. But to leave Croix-aux- Bois and again cross the forest was not to be thought of, for Mme. Keller's state would not allow of such a thing. It was lucky that we had fallen into such good French hands as the Stengers'.

The Stengers were peasants in comfortable circumstances, and seemed pleased to be able to render a service to their countrymen in distress. I need not say we said nothing about the nationality of Jean Keller. That would have complicated matters.

The 15th of September ended without an alarm, and on the 16th there was nothing to justify the fears Hans Stenger had inspired us with.

Even during the night we heard no firing at the back of the Argonne. Perhaps the Imperialists did not know that the Croix-aux-Bois defile was clear; in any case, as its narrowness would be a serious obstacle for the march of a column with its transport, it would be better to try and force the passages of Grand Pre or Islettes. We therefore regained hope. Besides, the rest and attention had already had their effect on Mme. Keller. Courageous woman! It was strength that failed her, not energy!

What a hound is fate! In the afternoon of the 16th suspicious characters began to appear in the village, stealers of fowls who went straight to the hen-roosts to begin with. There were men-thieves among them doubtless; but it was easy to see they were of German nationality, and that most of them were spies.

To our great alarm, M. Jean had to hide himself. As this seemed strange to Stengers, I had almost decided to tell them everything, when about four o'clock Hans came in exclaiming: "The Austrians! The Austrians!"

Many thousand men in white coats and shakos, with a high plate and a double-headed eagle, were coming in by the defile from the village of Boult. Doubtless their spies had told them the road was free. Who could say if the whole invasion would not come by this road?

At the shout from Stenger, M. Jean had appeared in the room where his mother lay.

I see him still. He was standing before the fire. He was waiting! What was he waiting for? Till every outlet was closed? But if he was taken prisoner by the Austrians, the Prussians would claim him, and that meant his death.

Mme. Keller rose on her bed.

"Jean!" she said, "you must go! Go this moment!"

"Without you, mother?"

135

"Without me! I will have it so."

"Escape, Jean!" said Mlle. Martha. "Your mother is mine! We will not abandon her."

"Martha!"

"I wish you to go!"

There was nothing for it but to go. The noise was increasing. Already the head of the column was spreading out into the village. Soon the Austrians would occupy Hans Stenger's house.

M. Jean embraced his mother. He gave Mlle. Martha a last kiss and disappeared.

And then I heard Mme. Keller murmur these words: "My son! My son! Alone in this country he does not know! Natalis — "

"Natalis!" repeated Mlle. Martha, pointing to the door. I understood what they expected of me. "Adieu!" I said.

A minute afterward I was out of the village.

CHAPTER XXI

Separated, after a three weeks' journey which a little more luck would have brought to a successful end! Separated, when a few leagues away there was safety for all! Separated, with the fear of never seeing each other again!

And these women abandoned in a peasant's hut, in a village occupied by the enemy, with only an old man of seventy to defend them!

In truth, ought I not to have kept with them? But thinking only of the fugitive in this terrible forest, which he did not know, could I hesitate to go with M. Jean, when I could be so useful to him? For M. de Lauranay and his companions there was only liberty at stake — at least I hoped so. For Jean Keller life was at stake! Nothing but this thought would have kept me back if I had been tempted to return to Croix-aux-Bois.

The reason this village had been occupied on the 16th of September was as follows: It will be remembered that of the five defiles through the Argonne, one only remained unoccupied by the French. But to guard against surprise, Dumouriez had sent to the entrance of this defile a colonel with two battalions and two squadrons; but this was too far away for Hans Stenger to know of their arrival. Such, however, was the conviction that the Imperialists would never risk themselves in this defile, that nothing was done to defend it. No abattis was made, no palisades erected. And imagining that there was no danger, the colonel had asked permission to send back some of his troops to head-quarters, and the permission had been given.

The Austrians, however, went to reconnoiter this passage, and hence the crowd of German spies who appeared at Croix-aux-Bois, and then the occupation of the defile. And that is how, owing to a miscalculation, one of the gates of the Argonne was left open.

As soon as Brunswick learned that the pass was free, he gave orders to occupy it. And this was done at the time when he was much hampered in the plains of Champagne, and was endeavoring to get up to Sedan so as to turn the Argonne from the north. But with the Croix-aux-Bois open, he could perhaps get through that way, and so he had sent an Austrian column with the emigres commanded by the Prince de Ligne, which surprised the French colonel, drove him back on Grand Pre, and seized the defile.

This happened just as we were about to take flight. Dumouriez, to repair his mistake, sent off General Chazot with two brigades, six squadrons, and four pieces of eight, to drive away the Austrians before they could intrench themselves.

Unfortunately, on the 14th, Chazot was not ready to attack, nor was he on the 15th, and when he tried on the evening of the 16th it was too late. He drove the Austrians from the defile and killed the Prince de Ligne, but he had to retire before superior forces. In spite of heroic efforts the passage of Croix-aux-Bois was definitely lost.

It was a regrettable mistake for France, and, I may add, for us, for if it had not been for this deplorable mistake on the 15th, we should have been among Frenchmen.

But now that was not possible. Chazot, seeing himself cut off from head-quarters, retreated on Vouziers, while Dubourg, who occupied Chene-Populeux, fearing to be surrounded, returned toward Attigny.

The French frontier was thus opened to the Imperial columns, and Dumouriez was in danger of being surrounded, and having to lay down his arms; and then there would be no serious obstacle to the advance of the invaders on Paris. As for us, Jeau Keller and I, we were in a bad way. Almost immediately after I left Stenger's house, I came up with M. Jean in the thick of the wood.

"You — Natalis?" he said.

"Yes, I!"

"And you promised never to leave my mother or Martha?"

"Stop a minute, Monsieur Jean. Listen to me!"

Then I told him all; how I knew this Argonne country and he did not, and how Mme. Keller and Mlle. Martha had, so to speak, ordered me to follow him, which I had not hesitated to do.

"And if I have done wrong, Monsieur Jean!" said I, "my Heaven punish me!"

"Come along, then!"

It would not do now to follow the defile to the frontier of the Argonne. The Austrians would have thrown themselves across the outlet of the Croix-aux-Bois and the Briquenay footpath. Hence we had to bear away to the north-west so as to strike the line of the Aisne.

We kept on in this direction until the light failed us. To keep on in the darkness was not possible. How could we make sure of our course! All we could do was to halt for the night.

In the earlier hours the sound of firing was incessant, and less than half a league away. These were the volunteers of Longwe trying to retake the defile from the Austrians. But not being in sufficient force they were obliged to disperse. Unfortunately, they did not retreat through the forest, where we would have run against them and ascertained that Dumouriez was at his head-quarters at Grand Pre. We would have accompanied them, and then, as I learned later, I would have rejoined my regiment, the Royal Picardy, which had left Charleville to join the army of the center. Once we got to Grand Pre we should have been among friends, and could have taken measures for the safety of those we had abandoned at Croix-aux-Bois.

But the volunteers had evacuated the Argonne, and ascended the course of the Aisne so as to regain head-quar- ters.

It was a dreary night. A cold drizzle fell, which soaked us to the bone. Our clothes, torn by the thorns, were in rags. I had not my frock with me. Our boots had become so worn that they almost fell off our feet. Were we to have to walk barefooted? It looked like it. We were quite chilled, for the rain filtered through the foliage on to us, and I sought in vain for a shelter. Every now and then we had an alarm; the firing, at times, got so close that I thought I could see the flash, and expected every moment to hear the Prussian cheers! And we had to fly further away for fear of being taken. How long the day seemed coming!

At dawn we renewed our run through the forest. I say run, for we went as fast as the ground permitted, while I took the direction the best I could from the rising sun. We had nothing inside us, and hunger began to pinch. M. Jean had had no time to bring food with him when he fled from the Stengers. I had come away like a madman, when I found that our retreat would be cut off by the Austrians, and was just as badly provisioned. Crows, sparrow- hawks, and numberless small birds, yellow-hammers chiefly, flew about us in the trees, but game there was little. Occasionally we caught sight of a hare or a couple or grouse running away under the brush-wood. But how could we catch them? Fortunately, chestnut - trees were not wanting in the Argonne, nor were chestnuts at this time of year. And I cooked a few in the ashes after lighting a fire of brush-wood with a little gunpowder. It was this only which prevented us dying of hunger.

The night came. The trees were so thick that we had only done three leagues since the morning. But the edge of the wood could not now be far off — two or three leagues at the outside. We could hear the musketry of the skirmishers along the Aisne. Twenty-four hours more and we should be on the other side of the river, perhaps at Vouziers, perhaps at one of the villages on the left bank.

I say nothing of our fatigue. We had no time to think of it. That night, although my brain was possessed with a thousand fears, I lay down to sleep at the foot of a tree. I remember that up to the time my eyes closed I thought of the regiment of Colonel von Grawert, which had left thirty of its men dead in the clearing a few days before.

In the morning I saw that M. Jean had not slept a wink. He hardly thought of himself — we know him well enough to be sure of that — but to think of his mother and Mlle. Martha in this house at Croix-aux-Bois in the hands of the Austrians, exposed to their insults, and outraged perhaps, almost drove him to desperation. In fact, during this night it was M. Jean who had kept guard. And I must have slept well, for the firing could still be heard close by, although it did not wake me, and M. Jean let me sleep on.

When we were starting, M. Jean said to me: "Natalis, listen to me!"

He said these words in the tone of a man who had finally made up his mind. I saw what he was driving at, and I answered without waiting for him.

"No, Monsieur Jean. I will not listen to you if you are going to talk of my leaving you."

"Natalis," continued he, "you are devoted to me, and so you came with me."

"Well?"

"While it was only a question of fatigue I said nothing. Now it is a question of peril. If I am taken and you are with me they will not spare you. That means death for you, Natalis, and that I can not accept. Go, then! Get over the frontier. I will try to do the same from my side, and if we do not meet again — "

"Monsieur Jean," said I, "it is time to get on our road. We shall be saved or die together."

"Natalis."

"I mean I will not leave you!"

And so we started. The early hours of the day were noisy. The artillery boomed amid the crackle of the musketry. It was another attack on the defile of Croix-aux- Bois — an attack which did not succeed in the face of a more numerous enemy.

About eight o'clock silence came over all. Not a single gunshot did we hear. Terrible uncertainty for us! That a battle had been fought in the defile, there could be no doubt. But what had been the result? Ought we to turn back into the forest? Instinct told us no. We must keep on toward Vouziers.

At noon a few chestnuts baked in the cinders gave us our only repast. The thickets were so dense that we hardly did four hundred yards an hour. And then there began again sudden alarms, shots to the right, the left, and at last the sound of the alarm bell in all the villages of the Argonne.

Evening came. We could not be a league from the Aisne. Next day, if no obstacle stopped us, we should be safe on the other side of the river. We had only to go down stream a short distance and we could cross by the bridges of Senuc or Grand Ham, which neither Glairfayt nor Brunswick had yet seized.

We had halted about eight o'clock. We were looking about for a shelter against the cold. All we could hear was the dripping of the rain on the leaves. All was quiet, and yet I know not why, the quiet made me feel uneasy.

Suddenly, not twenty yards away, we heard voices. M, Jean seized me by the hand.

"Yes," said some one; "we have been on his track since he left Croix-aux-Bois!"

"He can not escape us."

"But nothing of the thousand florins to the Austrians!"

"Not a word, comrades!"

I felt M. Jean's hand clasp mine.

"Buch's voice!" he whispered in my ear.

"The blackguards!" said L "There are five or six of them probably! Do not wait for them!"

And we slipped away through the thicket. Suddenly a branch broke, and the noise betrayed us. Immediately a flash of light illuminated the underwood. We had been seen.

"Come, Monsieur Jean, come!" I exclaimed.

"Not till I have settled one of them!" he said.

And he fired his pistol at the group which was coming after us.

I think one of the vagabonds fell, but I had something else to do than to stop and see. We ran as fast as our legs could carry us. I felt Buch and his comrades at our heels. We were nearly exhausted.

A quarter of an hour afterward, the band fell on us. There were half a dozen armed men.

In a moment we were knocked down, tied by the hand, and then pushed up and driven along with many blows.

An hour afterward we were in the hands of the Austrians at Longwe, and safe under guard at a house in the village.

CHAPTER XXII

Was it chance that had put Buch on our track? I think so. But we learned afterward that since our last meeting the younger Buch had never given up the search, not so much to avenge his dead brother as to secure the thousand florins. He had lost our track when we entered the Argonne, but he had found it again at Croix-aux-Bois. He was one of the spies who appeared on the afternoon of the 16th, and had recognized M. and Mlle, de Lauranay at the Stengers'. He learned that we had only just left. We could not be far off. Half a dozen of his cronies joined him and he set off in pursuit. We know the rest.

Now that we were guarded in a way to prevent all escape, and were waiting till our fate was decided — which would not take long, and was not very doubtful — all we had to do was to write to our friends, as they say.

At first, I examined the room which served for our prison. It occupied half the ground-floor of a low house. Two windows, opposite to each other, admitted the light, one from the road, one from a yard. We should probably go forth from this house to die: M. Jean under the double charge of having struck an officer and deserting in time of war; I for complicity and probably as a spy, owing to my being a Frenchman.

I heard M. Jean murmur: "It is the end this time!"

I said nothing! I must confess that my confidence had received a severe shaking, and the position seemed desperate.

"Yes, the end!" said M. Jean. "But what would it matter if my mother and Martha and those we love were out of danger! But, after us, what will become of them? Are they still in the village in the hands of the Austrians?"

And if they had not been taken away, they were not very far from us. It is hardly a league and a half between Croix-aux-Bois and Longwe.

It was to be hoped the news of our arrest had not reached them!

That is what I was thinking of, and what I feared more than anything. It would be death to Mme. Keller. I hoped the Austrians had taken them to the advance posts beyond the Argonne. Perhaps Mme. Keller could hardly be moved! And if they forced her to take to the road! If there was no one to look after her!

The night passed. Our position was unchanged. What sad thoughts come into the mind when death is near!

Then it is that our whole life passes in a moment before our eyes.

We were very hungry, having lived on chestnuts for the last two days. The guard never thought of bringing us any food. We were worth a thousand florins to Buch, and he might have fed us well at that price!

We had not seen him again, it is true. Doubtless he had gone to report his capture to the Prussians. I thought that would take him some time. We were in Austrian hands, but it would be Prussians who would decide our fate. They would come to Croix-aux-Bois, whence they would take us to head-quarters. That would mean delay unless the order for execution came to Longwe. Whatever they might do they would not let us die of hunger.

About seven o'clock next morning the door opened and a sutler in a blouse appeared with a bowl of soup with bread soaked in it. The quantity took the place of quality. We had no right to be dainty, and I was so hungry that I set to work ravenously.

I should have liked to question this sutler, to ask him what was the news at Longwe, and at Croix-aux-Bois; if they were talking of the approach of the Prussians, if their intention was to take this defile in crossing the Argonne; in fact, how things stood generally. But I did not know enough German to be understood or understand. And M. Jean, deep in his reflections, kept silence. I did not like to disturb him. And it was thus impossible to talk with the man.

Nothing new occurred during the morning. We were kept in sight all the time; but were allowed to walk backward and forward in the little yard, where the Austrians examined us with rather more curiosity than sympathy as you may suppose. I put a good face on it, and walked about with my hands in my pockets, whistling the most lively marches of the Royal Picardy.

Should I not have said to myself: "Go on, whistle away, poor blackbird in your cage. They will soon cut short your whistle!"

At noon we had another bowl of soup and soaked bread. Our bill of fare was not varied, and I began to regret the chestnuts of the Argonne. But we had to make the best of it. All the more for our weasel-faced sutler giving us a look which said as plainly as possible, "It is much too good for you!" I would cheerfully have thrown the basin at his head. But it was better to get up our strength so as not to fail at the last moment.

I got M. Jean to share my meager repast with me. He understood my reasons and eat a little. He was thinking of something else, though. His mind was away in the house of Hans Stenger with his mother and his betrothed. He muttered their names, he called them! Sometimes, in a sort of delirium, he moved toward the door as if to rejoin them. And then he fell back, and if he did not weep, he was all the more terrible to look at, and tears would have comforted him. But no! and my heart bled for him.

Meanwhile files of soldiers went by, marching at ease; then came columns through Longwe. The trumpets were silent; so were the drums. The enemy was going off silently to the line of the Aisne. Thousands of men must have gone by. Were they Austrians or Prussians, I much wanted to know. There was only one report of a gun in the east of the Argonne. Then the gate of France must be wide open? They could not be defending it.

About ten o'clock in the evening a detachment of soldiers appeared in our room. This time they were Prussians. And, to my horror, I

146

recognized the uniform of the Leib regiment come to Longwe after the engagement with the volunteers in the Argonne.

They tied our hands behind us and made us go out.

M. Jean addressed the corporal who commanded the party.

"Where are you taking us?" he said.

The only reply from this brute was a blow that sent us staggering into the road.

We looked like poor beggars going to execution without trial. But I had not been taken with arms in my hand! Tell that to these savages? They would have laughed in my face!

We followed the road from Longwe toward the edge of the Argonne, which bends of a little beyond the village on the way to Vouziers. In about five hundred yards we stopped in the center of a clearing where the Leib regiment had been encamped. A few minutes afterward we were brought before Colonel von Grawert.

He contented himself with looking at us without saying a word. Then he turned on his heel, gave the signal for departure, and the regiment began to march.

I understood from this that we would have to appear before a court-martial, that a few forms were needed before they administered a dozen pills to our stomach, and that that would have taken place immediately if the regiment had stopped at Longwe. But things, it seemed, were pressing, and the Imperialists had no time to lose if they were to drive the French from the Aisue.

In fact, Dumouriez, having learned that the Imperialists were masters of the defile of Croix-aux-Bois, hit upon another plan. This consisted in descending the left boundary of the Argonne to the defile of Islettes and there backing up against Dillon who occupied it. In this way our soldiers would be face to face with the columns of Clairfayt, who was advancing from the frontier, and with those of Brunswick on the French side. He was prepared, in fact, to see the Prussians get through the Argonne so as to cut the road to Chalons as soon as he struck the camp at Grand Pr6.

Silently he evacuated his head-quarters on the night of the 15th of September. After crossing the two bridges over the Aisne he halted on the heights of Autry, four leagues from Grand Pre. Thence, notwithstanding two panics which threw his troops into disorder, he advanced to Dammartin-sur-Hans so as to reach the positions at Saint Menehould, which are at the end of the defile of Islettes.

At the same time, as the Prussians would debouch from the Argonne through the defile of Grand Pre, he took precautions that the camp at Epine, on the Chalons road, should not be carried if the enemy attacked it instead of turning aside to fight him at Saint Menehould.

Generals Beurnoville, Chazot and Dubouquet received orders to rejoin Dumouriez, and Kellermann was ordered to hasten his march.

If all three generals were at the rendezvous to time, Dumouriez would have with him more than thirty-five thousand men, and could make a stand against the Imperialists.

Brunswick and his Prussians had begun to hesitate after definitely fixing their plan of campaign. At last they decided to cross by the Grand Pre, debouch from the Argonne so as to seize the Chalons road, and surround the French army at Saint Menehould.

That was why the Leib regiment had so hurriedly left Longwe, and why we were going toward the Aisne. The weather was frightful; it was foggy, and it rained. The roads were broken up; the mud covered us up to the waist. To march in this way, with arms strapped behind us, was torture; in fact they would have done better to have shot us on the spot.

And this Frantz von Grawert who ten times came and attacked us to our faces! M. Jean ground in vain at his cords to get his hands free and strangle the lieutenant there and then!

We struck the Aisne and kept along its bank. We had to wade the Dormoise, Tourbe, and Bionne brooks. We never stopped, our object being to arrive in time to occupy the heights of Saint Menehould. But we did not go very fast. Frequently we stuck in the mud.

At ten o'clock rations were served out, and as the Prussians went short, you may guess how it fared with the two prisoners they dragged along with them like beasts.

We could hardly speak. Every time we said anything we were saluted with a blow. Our guards probably wished to please Frantz von Grawert, and they succeeded only too well.

This night of the 19th of September was one of the worst we had passed. We regretted our halts under the trees in the Argonne when we were-still fugitives. Before it was daylight we reached a sort of marsh on the left of Saint Menehould. There the camp was pitched in a couple of feet of mud. No fire was lighted, for the Prussians did not wish to announce their presence.

At length day dawned — the day, doubtless, of battle. Perhaps the Boyal Picardy was there, and I should not be in the ranks with my comrades!

There was much going to and fro in the camp. Orderlies and aids-de-camp were flying across the marsh every instant. The drums beat, the trumpets sounded. There was a sound of firing on the right.

The French had outstripped the Prussians in the race to Saint Menehould!

It was nearly eleven o'clock when a file of soldiers came in search of M. Jean and me. At first they took us to a tent where half a dozen officers were seated, presided over by Colonel von Grawert. Yes! he presided at the court- martial in person!

It did not take long. It was a simple formality to establish our identity. Jean Keller, already sentenced to death for striking an officer, was again condemned for desertion, and I was condemned as a French spy!

There was no good in disputing the matter, and when the colonel added that the execution would take place at once —

"Vive la France!" said I. "Vive la France!" echoed Jean Keller.

CHAPTER XXIII

It certainly seemed to be finished this time. The muskets were practically now pointing at us. They were only waiting for the word to fire. Well, Jean Keller and Natalis Delpierre knew how to die!

Outside the tent was the platoon that was to shoot us — a dozen men of the Leib regiment under the orders of a lieutenant.

They had not untied our hands. Why not? We could not escape. A few steps perhaps, and against a wall or at the foot of a tree we should fall under the Prussian bullets! Ah! what would I not have given to have died in fair fight with twenty sword-cuts, or shot in two by a can- non-ball! To receive your death without being able to defend yourself is very hard!

We marched along in silence, M. Jean thinking of Martha he would never again see, of his mother whom this last blow would kill.

I thought of my sister Irma, of my other sister Firminie, of all that were left of our family! I saw my father, my mother, my village, all I loved, my regiment, my country.

Neither of us took any notice of where the soldiers were taking us. What did it matter? We were to be killed like dogs!

Evidently as I am telling you this story, and have written it with my own hand, I must somehow have escaped. But I never thought then what was to be the end of this history!

About fifty yards from the tent we had to pass through the Leib regiment. All of them knew Jean Keller. Not one of them showed a sign of pity for him-the pity that is never refused to those about to die! What natures! they are well worthy of being commanded by Yon Gra- werts! The lieutenant saw us. He looked at M. Jean, who looked at him: with one it was the satisfaction of a hatred nothing could quench, with the other it was scorn. For a moment I thought the wretch was coming with

151

us. In truth I wondered if he was going to command the firing party! But a trumpet-call was heard, and he disappeared among the soldiers.

We then turned off round one of the knolls that the Duke of Brunswick had just occupied. These heights command the small town and surround it for three quarters of a league. At their foot runs the road to Chalons. The French were in position on the neighboring ridges.

Below us were numerous columns ready to attack our positions so as to command Saint Menehould. If the Prussians succeeded, Dumouriez would be in difficulties in face of an enemy his superior in numbers.

In clear weather I could have recognized the French uniforms on the heights, but all was hidden in a thick fog which the sun had not yet dissipated. We could hear a few guns, but we could scarcely see the flashes.

Believe me, I still had hope, or rather I forced myself, not to despair. But what chance of help was there on the side we were? All the troops called in by Dumouriez were with him round Saint Menehound, were they not?

It was about a quarter past eleven. The noon of September 20th would never strike for us.

We had reached our destination. The platoon left the main road to Chalons on the left. The fog was still too thick for objects to be visible a hundred yards away. It could be felt, however, that the fog would soon disappear.

We were in a little wood, chosen as the place of execution, from which we were never to return.

In the distance we heard the roll of the drums, the call of the trumpets, the heavy boom of the artillery, and the crackle of the musketry.

I tried to make out what it all meant, as if that could interest me at such a time! I observed that these sounds of battle came from the right, and seemed to be getting nearer to us. Was an engagement in progress on the Chalons road? Had a column made a sortie from the camp at Epine and taken the Prussians on the flank? I could not make it out.

If I have told you this with a certain precision, it is that you may know what was my state of mind. The details are graven on my memory. Besides, we do not forget such things. For me it is all as if it took place yesterday.

We had just entered the little wood. A hundred paces off the firing party stopped before an abattis of trees.

This was where we were to be shot.

The officer in command — a hard-faced man — gave the word to halt. The soldiers formed up, and I still hear the rattle of their muskets on the ground.

"This is the place," said the officer.

"All right," said Jean Keller.

He answered in a firm voice, with his head held high, and his look unquailing.

And then coming to me he spoke in that language of France he loved so well, and which I was to hear for the last time.

"Natalis," he said, "we are going to die! My last thought will be for my mother, and after her for Martha, whom I love best in the world. Poor women! May Heaven have pity on them! As to you, Natalis, forgive me — "

"What have I to forgive, Monsieur Jean?"

"It is I — "

"Monsieur Jean," I replied, "I have nothing to forgive. What I have done has been freely done, and I would do it again! Let me embrace you! and let us die like brave men!"

We fell into eacb other's arms.

And never shall I forget Jean Keller's bearing when he turned to the officer and said in a voice without a tremble: "At your orders!"

The officer made a sign. Four soldiers stepped out from the platoon, touched us on the back, and guided us to the foot of the same tree. We were to die together. It was best so!

I remember that this tree was a beech. I see it now with a broad scar of peeled bark. The fog began to rise, and other trees began to come out of the mist.

M. Jean and I stood upright, hand in hand, looking the platoon in the face.

The officer stepped back a little. The click of the locks, as the muskets were brought to the ready, is still in my ears. I squeezed Jean Keller's hand, and I tell you on my oath his did not tremble in mine.

The guns were brought up to the shoulder. At the first word of command they would drop to the aim, at the second they would fire, and all would be over. Suddenly there was a noise in the wood behind the soldiers.

Heavens! What did I see? Mme. Keller, bome up by Mlle. Martha and my sister Irma! Her voice I could hardly hear. Her hand waved a paper, and Mlle. Martha, my sister, and M. de Lauranay shouted with her: "They are French! They are French!"

At this instant there was a loud report, and I saw that Mme. Keller had fainted.

Neither M. Jean nor I had fallen. Was it not our platoon that had fired?

No! Half a dozen of them lay dead on the ground, while the officer and the rest were running off at full speed.

At the same time on every side through the woods I heard the shouts I still hear: "En avant! En avant!"

154

It was the shout of the French, and not the croaking "Vorwarts "of the Prussians!

A detachment of our soldiers had been thrown out across the Chalons road and had reached the wood just in time. Their fire had just preceded that of the platoon, and settled matters as we see. But how was it they had arrived in the nick of time? That I knew later on.

M. Jean leaped to his mother, whom Mlle. Martha and my sister were holding up. The unhappy woman, thinking the firing had been our deaths, had fainted quite away.

But under the kisses of her son she revived, and returned to herself with these words on her hps: "French! He is French!"

What did she want to say? I hurried to M. de Lauranay. He could not speak.

Mlle. Martha took the paper which Mme. Keller held so tightly, and gave it to M. Jean.

I see the paper now. It was a German journal, the "Zeitblatt."

M. Jean took it! He read it. Tears flowed down his cheeks. Heavens! One is fortunate to be able to read under such circumstances!

And then the same word escaped from his lips. He rose. He looked like a man who would suddenly go mad. What he would have said I could not understand, so much was his voice choked by emotion.

"French! I am French!" he exclaimed. "Ah, mother! Martha! I am a Frenchman!"

Then he fell on his knees in a burst of thankfulness to God.

But Mme. Keller rose.

"And now, Jean, they will no longer force you to fight against France!"

"No, mother! It is now my right and my duty to fight for her!"

CHAPTER XXIV

M. Jean dragged me away without stopping to explain. We were with the French, who came swarming out of the wood, and we marched toward the cannon which began to roll continuously.

I tried to think. How could Jean Keller, the son of M. Keller, a German by birth, be a Frenchman? I could not understand it! All I could say was that he would fight like one!

But now I must say something about what had happened on this morning of the 20th of September, when a detachment of our soldiers found themselves in the wood on the Chalons road at such a lucky moment for us.

It will be remembered that in the night of the 16th Dumouriez had left the camp at Grand Pre for the position at Saint Menehould, where he had arrived next day, after a march of four or five leagues.

In front of Saint Menehould were several hills, separated by deep ravines. Their base is defended by the quagmires and marshes formed by the Aure where it joins the Aisne.

The heights on the right are those of Hyron, facing the Lune hills; on the left they are those of Gizaucourt. Between them and Saint Menehould is a sort of flat marshy plain, through which runs the road to Chalons. This plain is varied by a few knolls of little importance, among others that of the mill of Valmy, which rises above the village of that name, which has become so celebrated since this 20th of September.

Since his arrival Dumouriez had occupied Saint Mene- hound, and touched hands with Dillon, who was ready to defend the defile of the Islettes against all comers trying to take the Argonne in reverse.

Kellermann, after the evacuation of the camp at Grand Pre, made a retrograde movement; and on the 19th was still two leagues from Saint

Menehould, when Beurnonville with nine thousand men of the auxiliary army was at the camp of Maulde.

Dumouriez intended that Kellermann should establish himself on the heights of Gizaucourt, which command those of La Lune, toward which the Prussians were marching. But the order had been misunderstood, and it was the plateau of Valmy which Kellermann occupied with General Valence and the Due de Chartres, who, at the head of twelve battalions of infantry and twelve squadrons of artillery, particularly distinguished himself in the battle.

Meanwhile Brunswick had arrived, in the hope of cutting the road to Chalons and driving Dillon from the Islettes. Saint Menehould, surrounded by twenty-four thousand men, in addition to the cavalry of the emigres, would soon bring Dumouriez and Kellermann to surrender.

And it was to be feared that this would be the case, for the heights of Gizaucourt were not in the hands of the French, as Dumouriez had intended. If the Prussians, already masters of the Lune hills, seized on the heights of Gizaucourt, their artillery could sweep the French positions.

The King of Prussia saw this. That was why, instead of marching on Chalons, he disregarded Brunswick's advice, and gave the order to attack, hoping to throw Dumouriez and Kellermann into the quagmires of Saint Menehould.

About half past eleven o'clock the Prussians began to descend the Lune hills in good order, and halted half-way.

It was at this moment, that is to say, at the beginning of the battle, that a Prussian column came up with Kellermann's rear-guard on the Chalons road. A few companies of this rear-guard had been thrown out through the little wood, and they had put to flight the platoon that was to have shot us.

And it was just then, when M. Jean and I were in the thick of the advance, that I discovered my comrades of the Royal Picardy.

"Delpierre?" shouted one of the officers of my squadron, catching sight of me just as the bullets began to play on our ranks.

"Here, captain!" said I.

"Come back to time, eh?"

"As you see; in time to fight!"

"But you are on foot?"

"Well, captain, I must fight on foot, and I shall not do badly."

They gave arms to each of us — M. Jean and myself — a musket and a sword apiece. We crossed the leathers on our chests, and if we were not in uniform it was because the regimental tailor had not had time to attend to us!

I should say that the French were repulsed at the beginning of the action, but the carabineers of General Valence came up in support, and order was re-established.

Meanwhile the fog, rent by the gun-flashes, had disappeared. We fought in bright sunshine. In the two hours twenty thousand discharges of artillery were exchanged between the heights of Valmy and those of La Lune. Twenty thousand, did I say? Good! say twenty-one thousand, and let it stand. Better hear that, as the proverb says, than be deaf!

At this time the position near the hill of Valmy was very difficult to hold. The artillery was cutting lanes in our troops. Kellermann's horse was shot. Not only did the Prussians hold the Lune hills, but they were trying to get possession of those of Gizaucourt. We held those of Hyron, it is true, but Clairfayt was trying to get at them with his twenty-five thousand Austrians; and if he succeeded, the French would be shattered back and front.

Dumouriez saw the danger. He sent Stengel with sixteen battalions to repulse Clairfayt, and Chazot, so as to occupy Gizaucourt before the

Prussians. Chazot arrived too late. The place was taken, and Kellermann had to defend Valmy against artillery which opened on him on all sides. A powder-wagon blew up near the mill and caused a moment's confusion. We were there, M. Jean and I, and it is a miracle we were not killed.

Then it was that the Due de Chartres came with the reserve of artillery, and cheerily replied to the guns on La Lune and Gizaucourt. The affair was getting warm. The Prussians, in three columns, moved on to the assault of the mill of Valmy to dislodge us and hurl us into the marsh.

I still see Kellermann, and I can hear him now. He gave orders to let the enemy advance to the crest of the hill before we charged him. We were ready; we waited. All that was wanted was to sound the charge.

Then, at the right moment, this cry escaped from Kellermann's lips: "Vive la Nation!"

"Vive la Nation!" we answered.

And we roared it out so that you could hear it above the roar of the guns.

The Prussians had reached the crest of the hill. With their columns well in line, their steady step, the coolness they showed, they were terrible to face. But the French dash swept them away. We threw ourselves on them. The slaughter was terrible.

Suddenly, amid the flashes of fire that darted around us, I saw Jean Keller with his sword on high. He had recognized one of the Prussian regiment* that we had begun to hurl from the slopes of Valmy.

It was Colonel von Grawert's regiment. Lieutenant Frantz was fighting with great courage, for it is not courage that German officers want!

M. Jean and Frantz von Grawert were face to face.

159

The lieutenant thought we had fallen under the Prussian bullets, and here he found us! You may guess his astonishment. But he had scarcely time to recognize us. "With a bound M. Jean was on him, and with his sword he hit him on the head.

The lieutenant fell dead, and I have always thought it was right that he should receive death at the hands of Jean Keller.

But the Prussians still tried to carry our position. They attacked us with extraordinary vigor. But we were too many for them, and by two o'clock they had ceased firing and returned to the plain.

But the battle was only suspended. At four o'olock the King of Prussia, marching at the head, again formed up three columns of attack with his best infantry and cavalry. Then our battery of twenty-four guns, stationed at the foot of the mill, cannonaded the Prussians with such violence that they could not climb the slope. Then the night came and they went back.

Kellermaun remained master of the plateau, and the name of Valmy rang through France, the very day that the Convention at its second sitting decreed the Republic.

CHAPTER XXV

We have reached the end of my story, which I might have called "The Story of a Leave in Germany."

That evening in a house in the village of Valmy, Mme. Keller, M. and Mlle, de Lauranay, my sister Irma, M. Jean, and I found ourselves together.

How great was our joy after such experiences! What passed between us you can guess.

"Wait a bit!" said I. "I am not curious, and I can remain with my beak in the water if you like — but I should like to know — "

"How it is, Natalis, that Monsieur Jean is your countryman?" said my sister.

"Yes, Irma, and it seems so strange to me that I am afraid you must have made a mistake — "

"We do not make such mistakes as those, my good Natalis," said M. Jean. And this is what he told me in a few words. At the village of Croix-aux-Bois, where we left M. de Lauranay and his companions guarded by Austrians, the Austrians were soon replaced by Prussians. This column had in its ranks a certain number of young men whom the levy of the 31st of July had torn from their families.

Among them was a lad named Ludwig Pertz, who came from Belzingen. He knew Mme. Keller and came to see her when he heard she was a prisoner of the Prussians. They told him what had happened to M. Jean, and how he had taken flight through the Argonne. And then Ludwig Pertz had exclaimed: "But your son has nothing to fear, Madame Keller! They had no right to embody him. He is not a Prussian! He is a Frenchman!"

You may guess how this declaration was received. Pertz being asked for his authority, presented Mme. Keller with a copy of the "Zeitblatt" containing a report of the lawsuit which on the 17th of August had at last come to an end. The decision was that the Kellers must lose their claim, it being necessary that army contracts should be given out only to Germans of Prussian birth; and it had been discovered that M. Keller's ancestors had never obtained naturalization, that therefore the said Keller was never a Prussian, and therefore the said Keller had nothing owing him by the State!

That was the decision! That M. Keller had remained French there could be no doubt, but that was no reason why he should not be paid his due! However, that was law in Berlin in 1792. I do not think M. Jean thought of an appeal. He gave up his cause as lost — quite lost. It was indisputable that he had had a French father and a French mother, and he could not be much more French! And if a baptism of fire was required, he had had one at Valmy.

After the communication from Pertz it was important to find M. Jean as soon as possible. His friends heard that he had been captured at Longwe and taken to the Prussian camp with your servant. There was not an hour to lose. Mme. Keller recovered her strength at the danger that menaced her son. After the departure of the Austrian column, accompanied by M. de Lauranay, Mlle. Martha, my sister, and guided by honest Hans Stenger, she left Croix-aux-Bois, traversed the defile, and reached Brunswick's cantonment the very morning they were going to shoot us.

We had just come out of |the tent where the court-martial was held when she presented herself.

In vain she appealed to the judgment which made Jean Keller a Frenchman. She was repulsed. She then followed us along the Chalons road — and you know what happened.

The position of the French after Valmy I can dismiss in a few words.

At first, during the night, Kellermann occupied the heights of Gizaucourt, and assured the position of the entire army.

The Prussians had, however, cut the road to Chalons and we could not communicate with the depots. But as we were masters of Vitry the convoys could come in as usual, and the army in camp at Saint Menehould did not run short.

The enemy's army remained in their cantonments until the last days of September. There were diplomatic advances which ended in nothing. The Prussians became anxious to pass the frontier. Provisions were failing them, sickness was making great ravages, and on the 1st of October the Duke of Brunswick decamped.

As the Prussians retired through the defiles of the Argonne we assisted them slightly, but not violently. They were allowed to retreat leisurely. Why, I do not know. Neither I nor many others understood the conduct of Dumouriez in the matter.

Doubtless there was some political reason for it, and as I said before, I do not understand politics.

The important fact is that the enemy repassed the frontier. It was done slowly, but it was done, and there was not a Prussian left in France — not even M. Jean, for he was out and out our countryman.

As soon after the departure as possible, in the first week of October, we returned together to our dear Picardy, when the marriage of Jean Keller and Martha de Lauranay took place. It will be remembered I was to be one of the witnesses at Belzingen, and you will not be surprised that I was one of the witnesses at Sauflieu. And if the marriage did not promise to be a happy one, there was never a marriage in this world that did.

As to me, I rejoined my regiment a few days afterward, I learned to read and to write, and became, as I have said, lieutenant, and then captain in the wars of the Empire.

That is my story, which I have written to put an end to those disputes among my friends at Grattenpache. If I have not spoken like a church book, I have told you the things as they happened. And now, readers, allow me to salute you with my sword.

Natalis Delpierre.

Captain of Cavalry,

(Retired List)

The End

Printed in Great Britain
by Amazon.co.uk, Ltd.,
Marston Gate.